Also by Rechan

Handcuffs & Lace
Will of the Alpha (editor)
Taboo (editor)
Will of the Alpha 2 (editor)
Will of the Alpha 3 (editor)
Dungeon Grind (co-editor)

Intimate Little Secrets

by Rechan

Intimate Little Secrets

Copyright © 2017 by Rechan

Cover illustration by Teagan Gavet

Published by FurPlanet Productions
Dallas, TX
http://www.FurPlanet.com

ISBN 978-1-61450-353-8

Printed in the United States of America
First Edition Trade Paperback 2017

TABLE OF CONTENTS

INTRODUCTION

Robert Baird

Rechan is a mole of many talents, and by now you've already seen one of them: he can pick a title like nobody's business. The elevator pitch is right there, right in the first word. And as you'd expect, he delivers in spades.

The stories here are alternately touching and titillating; tantalizing and tender. They invite us to explore the inner lives of characters consistently defined firstly by their refreshing believability. His gift for those small, intimate glimpses into their worlds is so genuine, and so skillfully executed, as to make every one of them a treasure.

Sometimes the scenario is Penthouse-letter pastiche, as in the chance and fortuitous late-night encounter that Marjani relates in "Strange on a Train." Sometimes it's all-too-real, like in the heart-breaking, heart-warming relationship "TLC" and its hard-won optimism. Trading between the wistful and the playful, Rechan offers up an array of characters that earn every second we spend with them.

Family gatherings, first encounters and life's biggest crises are on offer. No matter which, these vibrant personalities never seem like stock figures or actors on a stage. His gift for detailing each moment and interaction with its foibles and rough edges make them all the more delightful.

Kintsugi is an old Japanese practice derived from

wabi-sabi, a philosophy that encourages us to embrace the imperfect. When a ceramic bowl shatters, a kintsugi artist doesn't try to hide the cracks. They fill them in with gold-bearing lacquer that highlights every crack and line. Through this delicate artistry, flaws are transformed into the most striking part of an object's beauty.

This is kintsugi writing, and Rechan is one of the world's best artisans. I've always loved that about his work. Even in fantastic settings, it never loses its own honesty about the characters it depicts. The turmoil that springs from the complex relationship of Conner, Beth and Janine ("Rickety V") is precious because it's so natural and organic, never taking the easy way out. And as Luis Rojas grapples with his past, and his ex, in "When the Paint Dries" the obvious rawness of his feelings begs us to hang on every step of his growth.

So the title is a perfect encapsulation of this gem of a book. It's intimate: Rechan never settles for triteness, coaxing our empathy so naturally we don't realize it until we're already hooked. It's little, finding strength and passion and tragedy in each brief microcosm. And it's secret: a window into the private dramas of an unforgettable cast too keenly rendered not to be real.

Alas they're not. But this, *Intimate Little Secrets*, is the next best thing.

FANSERVICE

"This is a bad idea. It's a disaster, and I look ridiculous."

Thankfully no one was in the ladies room to hear Robin talking to herself, let alone see her, as it was two hours after everyone else had left the office. Everyone except her and Dean. Dean was why she was about to make a fool of herself.

She shook her head and tugged at the costume again. "I am just no Veronica Tamas." The actress who played Beretta St. James, the lead in *Tech-Trackers*. Part of the problem was Tamas, as a deer, had wonderful legs put on display by the mini-dress length lab coat and the sleek knee high black boots. With the longer torso and shorter limbs of a mink, Robin wasn't pulling it off.

At least they both had the same moderate bust and lean body, emphasized by the tight, fully buttoned lab coat, and maybe her butt was acceptable? Granted Tamas had the little teardrop tail, so you could see it, whereas her fluffy brush got in the way. Her mocha fur was "passable" for the more reddish bark of the deer's fur, but Robin's plain black hair couldn't match Tamas's rich mahogany and red streaked locks.

Thankfully the character's hair style changed every other season; Robin was not going to cut her hair to the saucy bob just for this, so she went with season three's ponytail, high on the back of her head. "I look like a stripper playing doctor," Robin said, adjusting the dark horned-rim glasses, and tried the St. James smirk in the mirror. Then she laughed and shook her head. The outfit was just ridiculous—no scientist would dress like this, especially not to go out hunting

9

the rogue nanomachines they had accidentally released. But then a scientist out fighting while dressed as a scientist was about as bonkers as the rest of the show.

Focusing on her appearance distracted her from the tight knot in her belly, and the fur crawling up on the back of her neck. She could just change back into her normal clothes and go home and forget all this.

But if she chickened out now, she'd never do it. Never forgive herself, either. That and all the effort of putting this stupid outfit together would have been wasted, and the accountant in her tolerated no waste.

"Robin this is not like you! This is…this is so messed up that I'm talking to myself in the third person."

Yet in a way it did fit her. Whenever she wanted something desperately enough, but no clear path to get them presented itself or when great risk stood in her way, Robin made a drastic charge head-first in hopes that by sheer force of will and luck things would come out all right. To get her first serious job out of college she called the hiring manager directly instead of going through typical channels. At age ten the desire to go to space camp consumed her, but she needed a science teacher's recommendation, which he kept forgetting. Finally she entered the science fair with all the body's organs painted on her swimsuit, and while she only made second place—stupid Willy Fenning and his stupid "How far do germs travel" project—all the judges wrote her glowing recommendations. The memory made her smile.

Here she was, looking across at a different kind of space camp. Dean was the latest in a long list of guys she had been too scared to talk to or too hesitant to declare her interest. The first step was always so terrifying.

Enough, no more. Time to gamble with something new and give that first step the finger. If he laughed at her, well she could just suck it up and move on, but at least she'd know she tried.

Either way Robin was tired of standing in the ladies room being scared.

She took a deep breath and pushed the bathroom door open, only to almost stumble when she walked out. Not used to wearing heels, she had to get the hang of walking in the boots. The added height was nice at least. With the palpable weight and swing when she stepped, the audible click-clack of the heels on the tile, and the way they encouraged her to move her hips, Robin actually felt a little sexy.

That feeling increased as she passed through Personnel, and was somewhere around her ribs when she entered the next room to hit the brick wall of anxiety.

Against the backdrop of silence, Robin could pick out where Dean sat by the absent tapping of his foot against the desk. She imagined his bronzed-blonde fur standing out from the dull hues of the room, the way he bobbed his head while waiting for the software to update on whichever terminal he sat at.

She had only noticed him last month when he fixed the computer at the desk next to hers. Most of that first week had been spent watching him without him noticing, but they had talked, even over lunch. Enough for her to spot the shy glances, the smiles and conversational discomfort that she often felt too. Still he hadn't picked up on the subtle hints she was interested in him, and Robin was tired of waiting for him to take the initiative. Well he couldn't ignore this declaration of interest. Was he too shy? Dean was straight—the Beretta St. James figurine on his desk told her that, but Robin had no idea if he was in a relationship. The thought made her freeze up. What if he was? Or was only into some other species? Was that why he hadn't gotten her nudges?

Robin looked around. She found the office's silent emptiness downright eerie; usually it bustled with the noise of keyboards tapping, phones beeping, and the quiet rustle of clothes on fur. Even at lunch time Faraji would eat at his desk, or others would take their lunch an hour later, so there were always people in the room. The stillness left her feeling vulnerable, like anyone could just step inside and see them.

She was stalling. Just do it.

Taking a swallow, she pushed further into the room, down the line, and stopped a couple of feet away. From here she could see the line of his side, the monitor's glow lighting his face in profile, and an earbud cord snaking down to his shirt pocket.

It was hard for Robin to dig into just what attracted her to Dean. Physically he was kind of cute, more in the boy-ish sweetness of his face, soft dark eyes, and the blonde-buff hue of his fur. That color was a fairly uncommon shade for a mink and thus fetching. She wanted to think that while they didn't watch or read the same things, those tastes shared a neighborhood; maybe if they talked more, there would be some real overlap. What she avoided acknowledging was the fact they were the same species, and her biology might just be coming to collect—something her mother loved to sink her teeth into and remind Robin of oh-so-often.

Robin struck what she thought was a suitably appropriate pose—fist on hip—and said, "Dean?"

No response. Oh right, the headphones. She said his name louder and got the same result. Robin snatched up an unused post-it stack and flung it at the back of his head. Direct hit!

First he jumped and glanced down at the post-its, then looked back at her just long enough to realize someone stood there. Fumbling with his shirt, Dean turned off the tPod and pulled the buds free. "Sorry," he said and turned more fully to face her.

Behind the thick lenses of his glasses, Dean's eyes bulged.

"Does it uh…Is this good?" Robin dropped a hand to the

belt around her waist, fiddling with it. Not wanting to go all the way and get an actual holster (or a gun for that holster), she'd clipped an old reading glasses sleeve to her belt.

"You look..." His mouth opened and closed, and he swiped his tongue out to wet it. "You look awesome."

In that moment she allowed herself to stop worrying about her appearance and actually *see* his face. In his eyes, in the curve of his cheeks, Dean looked at her like like other men looked at attractive women. He was staring like he hoped there would be more of her, like he wanted to drink her image like a fine art piece at a museum. Seeing that sent a rush fluttering through her, and Robin's ears burned. Everywhere unclenched and she beamed. "Really?"

"Yeah...There are a few things that aren't perfect but you're really doing all right." He glanced away, then stood up. "So, are you going to a costume party or something? Going to a convention?"

"Not, uh, not really, no."

Dean tilted his head. "Okay. Wait, I thought you didn't even like the show?"

"I don't." She stepped closer and her eyes dropped. "But you do."

His whiskers twitched. "Well yeah, I do but—oh." The implication registered across his face, and his tail flicked. "That's-that's uh, does that mean...are you liking me? Do you like me?" The way he looked was just about how Robin felt about five minutes ago.

"Yeah," she said with a little chuckle, looking away. "You weren't picking up my interested hints, and you weren't doing anything about it, so I thought...."

"There were hints? Erf. I thought you were just being nice. So, can we go out? Not now, but just in general?"

Robin smiled with what she thought was allure, and half-lid her eyes.

For a moment Dean stared at her, cocking his head. "Uh, is there something in your eye?"

"No, no I'm fine." Okay, so she was not good at the sexy look. Instead she thought back to the paranormal romance books she liked to read, trying to find something witty and coquettish. Ah! "So, if I said yes, what would you do?"

"Probably say or do something really stupid. Yeah, yeah definitely that."

"You're doing fine so far," she said.

Dean chuckled and came closer. "That's because we only just started."

A silence seeped in between them, not uncomfortable but charged with a tension, giving a feeling like something was going to happen next but she didn't know what. Robin wanted it happen though, whatever it was.

Dean reached out, his hand moving close to her upper arm. Then, before he made contact, he pulled back, like maybe he thought she was electric. Robin grabbed his wrist, then pulled his hand onto her shoulder.

Their gazes touched.

For a moment Dean only squeezed her shoulder, then his digits inched up to graze her throat. A faint chirr bubbled up as he stroked her so-soft fur, and she reached out to caress his wrist and forearm.

When his touch moved up to her cheek and muzzle, Robin closed her eyes and tilted into it, a soft breath escaping from her. The scent of him drew her in, her body easing closer to his until they bumped.

That caress lasted only a moment longer before he cupped her cheek, her whiskers brushed his, and she instinctively moved into the oncoming kiss.

Their teeth knocked together.

Robin yanked back, her eyes popping open, and a startled chuckle bubbled up between them.

Still he came in a second time and she had to give him points for the courage. He nipped her jaw once and then they were kissing for real. Letting her eyes close again, Robin sank into the kiss, although it was tentative and gentle, which was very all right with her. The warmth of his breath puffed across her muzzle, bringing her to smile against his lips.

It felt like they stood there for a blissful forever, caressing with their lips, inhaling little tastes of one another's scent at such an intimate distance. The tremble of a chirr had built up mutually and their mouths vibrated together. Robin finally put her hands on his shoulders, one of his went to pet along her side leisurely.

It wasn't clear which of them had started it or when, but the kiss deepened, muzzles rolling in little circles, one of them nudging their face against the other, then the other would push back. Dean's hand slid from her side to the small of her back, and she arched, rubbing her front against his. That's when she realized how into it they were getting, and how far the warmth had spread through her belly and down.

During all this they must have gradually migrated backwards because Robin's tail first brushed up against a cubicle wall, and then her shoulders propped against it. When Dean leaned into her, she yielded and braced against the wall—and it shifted behind her with a rattling wobble.

They broke apart with a gasp and a stumble. Papers and other office detritus either tumbled to the floor or jarred in place, but they were far enough from the end that the whole wall didn't come crashing down.

Dean broke into the momentary silence. "Maybe we should sit down."

"Good idea," Robin said.

He sat in the chair and Robin moved to settle on his lap— the chair rolled to bang into the desk behind it while she teetered wildly. Sputtering a laugh, Robin said, "Okay, I guess that's not going to work either."

"Hold on." Dean stood and slid some of the desk debris to one side, and scooted a few of the heavier, obstinate objects out of the way. He turned to her and patted the top of the desk, smiling.

Well, it lacked the pinache of a real "shove everything off the desk in a moment of passion" move, but she'd take it.

Still Robin paused. The interruption had sucked some of the sexy spell out of the atmosphere, forcing her to regroup. Was this really the best place to do this? What was she expecting here, how far was she looking to go? What did Dean think of her, throwing herself at him like this, and if she didn't stop, would he think less of her? Would it mess everything up?

Hesitation crept into Dean's excited, hopeful expression until it frayed into anxious doubt.

For once, Robin decided that she didn't care enough to stop. This had all been a gamble, so she was going to let it ride.

She flashed at smile she hoped looked alluring, but this time with no attempt at bedroom eyes. Dean's face bloomed into an excited grin that sent her into an inward victory dance—she was beautiful, he wanted her, and she wasn't lame or undesirable. A thought gnawed on the tail of her celebration—was he just excited because he was a horny guy? Was he even interested in Her?

Robin threw that thought in a cellar and locked the door. No, no doubts were going to spoil this.

The mink crossed and perched her bottom on the edge of the desk. Though even as he moved closer, she struggled to find a good place to put her tail—the desk was still crowded and she'd likely pinch it against her body if tucking it under, so she curled the fluffy brush around his legs when he pressed against her.

Instead of diving in again, he nipped her cheek, then her

jaw. His pointy teeth pricked but didn't threaten the thick hide under her pelt. Another nip glanced off her neck, she tilted her head back, and he dotted her throat with gentler bites and kisses. A chirring rumble trickled out of her, stuttered by his teeth. He made his way back to her muzzle and she got him on the chin, tugging playfully.

After his mouth found her again, Robin gripped his shoulders and pulled him tight, meshing their whiskers in a deeper kiss. First wetting his lips with her tongue, she pushed it inside—only enough to flirt against him, then to draw back, successfully luring his into her mouth to play with. This time when their bodies slid against one another, she felt Dean's erection against her stomach before he tilted his hips back, hiding it from her.

If she wanted, they could have sex here. No one would catch them, the janitor's scent lingered in the air from maybe an hour before, and any smell of sex would have long since dispersed by morning. Hell, the enticing aroma was already beginning to spice the air. The sheer inappropriateness of that realization sent a thrill through her body. It would be the most adventurous thing Robin had ever done.

Dean's hand drifted from her shoulder to merely nudge the edge of her breast. Leaning her shoulders back and making space, she cupped his hand and pressed it over her chest.

He needed no further prompting. Any fledgling doubts she had that his hesitancy came from maybe being too inexperienced was brushed away by the skill he used to roll her breast between his fingers and fluttered his thumb against the nipple that perked against her labcoat. She was glad she'd taken her bra off when she changed; no second layer to dull the sensation of his claw as it dimpled the skin of her areola.

The confidence radiated from his touches, showing he had only been waiting for her to green-light where they could go. He was eager for this, eager for her. With confidence came more courage and his other hand rubbed over her stomach, then down across her thigh, and she pressed into it. One of his fingers slid in between two buttons to brush the silky fur across her belly. Her ticklish giggle and jerk tore the kiss apart.

She punched him in the arm, but couldn't help smiling at the sight of him grinning like a boy who just told his first dirty joke.

Dean took a moment to look over her, his eyes sparkling in amusement.

"Penny for your thoughts?" she chirred, reaching out to brush nails through the fur of his neck. Oh, she had a good idea what lurked behind his hungry eyes, but the delight was in hearing him say it.

"Uh uh—it's really dorky and you'll laugh at me if I tell you."

"Yes, I probably will," she said, grinning, "but now I really want to know, so I won't hold it too hard against you."

He closed his eyes, probably not wanting to see her expression. "Sometimes, when I've watched the show and stuff…I've wondered what kind of underwear she'd wear. With the outfit." His fingers gave a delicate tug at the lab coat for emphasis.

It was a good thing his eyes stayed closed because while she didn't laugh, Robin winced and grinned at the same time. Still she shifted to press against the touch of his fingers, and when he opened his eyes, she said with as much husk as she could, "Well if you keep watching maybe you'll find out." A pause. "I mean, not the show, but keep looking." Ugh, that sounded better in her head. Along with stupid, how did that sound? Even as she doubted, she blushed, but the warmth spread down her body in a wave.

Both of Dean's hands came down to press along the outsides of her thighs. She readied for a kiss when he leaned in, but instead his muzzle dipped under hers and the fur of her throat tingled under his tongue, then his teeth, and she shivered all the way down. His hands smoothed over her bare lower thighs to rub the fur almost against the grain, making her squirm, his grasp shifting from the sides to the tops and then sliding higher. Instead of moving them under the "skirt" of the coat, they went over and opened the lowest button.

He tried to open up the inches bared by the labcoat but something stopped it. After several little tugs, he pulled away and they both glanced down.

The stupid freaking belt was in the way, holding her coat closed.

With a frustrated hiss she wrestled with it and snapped it off, before planting her hands on the table behind her and arching her back, presenting her stomach to him. Robin hoped she looked sexy and not dumb or desperate.

Instead of opening the coat up, Dean popped another one of the buttons. This time he slid it slowly free while watching her face. She smiled back and reached out to stroke over his chest.

Parting the coat with care, Dean exposed her stomach, thighs, and the front panel of her underwear.

"Well, I knew it'd be black. But this doesn't tell me anything. It seems I'll just have to look closer."

Robin smirked—and when his fingers grazed her belly, she growled, ""Oh if you tickle me, I will so bite your fingers."

He made a show of lifting his fingers up, while petting her stomach with his palm, smoothing down the fur to rub her thighs. There was no hiding her scent now, and pressing her thighs together told her she was damp.

He slid his hands up under the coat and around back, cupping her butt. Tensing her cheeks under his touch, she couldn't help but squirm as he traced the thong strap that slipped down the middle of her rear.

A grin split Dean's face. "A very, very fine choice."

It had been simple for her: if women's fashion had taught Robin anything, it was that sexy clothes were uncomfortable, and thongs are quite uncomfortable so they must be sexy. She hadn't expected this to go so far that he'd actually see them, so she picked them to help her feel sexy.

Dean squeezed her butt again, making her squirm, and he leaned in to run his tongue across her throat.

Some small part of her picked up on his own excited musk, but it was too muted, and she became aware of a desire to smell him; it rushed up through her, and the brush of his bulge against her leg spurred Robin on reach down and open his pants. Dean froze, then pulled back with eyes wide behind his glasses to watch as she parted his khakis and reached inside. The smell came before she touched it, a thick and intoxicating scent that made her tail shiver and whiskers fan out.

The smell intensified as she gripped his hard-on and dragged it out of his pants. From her grip she knew it wasn't that big—not that she'd ever had experience with large ones to compare—but the sight of it made her flush as hot as the skin in her hand, and also feel dirty in a bad way.

Despite that bolt of shame, Robin opened her legs and pulled him closer by his erection. She wanted to feel him against her, wanted his arms around her. With one hand she squeezed him, and with the other she hugged his neck, pulling him in for another kiss.

Dean obliged her, working his muzzle into her own again, breath steaming across her cheek. She filled his mouth with her tongue and wrestled. As the kiss intensified, and with him pressing against her—pushing on her really—she leaned back on the desk. She ended up sitting on his hands. Once he tugged them free he clutched her outer thigh and braced the small of her back.

Robin's shoulders ended up against the wall. She let go of his hard-on and brought her hand down to brace on the tabletop. Dean leaned over her, their bodies crushed tight, and she could feel the heat and hardness of him grinding into her belly.

With a wet huff he pulled from the kiss, dropped his muzzle down and bit her shoulder through the coat. Robin hissed out a moan and dug her claws into his nape, pulling his mouth tight into her neck. When his teeth found her throat again, harder this time, all she could do was gasp and grip his hips with her thighs.

Yes, she wanted him, she let him know in the way her back arched and she pushed against his erection, her stomach fluttering, in the way her teeth caught his ear and pulled on it before she groaned into it. In that moment Robin decided they were going to have sex at work, this was going to happen.

Wait, she didn't bring any condoms. Never having expected it to go this far, she hadn't brought any. It wasn't time for her season, most likely, but still that was so risky. Did he have any? Would he settle for oral? No matter what, they were going to have fun.

Fate chose that moment to have Dean come on her stomach.

He jerked, his breath stuttering through his nose, and a warm wetness started to spread through the labcoat. For a moment she wasn't sure what was happening, thought something was terribly wrong when his mouth broke its hold on her throat and he groaned.

Then she felt it, the throb of his erection, the way he rubbed himself against her, and knew what happened. Oh no.

Before he finished leaking, Dean pulled away, a few stray strings connecting them, and they could see the mess of his stuff staining her exposed stomach in a fat puddle. Some of it had definitely gotten onto the labcoat, and a few smears seeped into his shirt. The smell was so thick, and despite herself it turned her on so much.

He said nothing, just buried his face in his hands, and at first she thought he was hyperventilating, but it was just the quick breath from their making out.

She had to do something now, but she couldn't just say it was okay, her gut told her that wouldn't do it. She needed to distract him, maybe. Go outside the box.

Reaching out she caressed the back of one concealing hand. "Dean, Dean look at me."

He opened his hands just enough to peek out at her, like a little boy at his first scary movie, not wanting to see what came next.

Robin swirled a finger in the mess on her belly, brought it up to her lips and put it in her mouth. She smiled around it and made eye contact. "Mmm." It was an effort to keep her expression warm and sexy—she had only tasted a guy's stuff a few times, and the musky salt of it left her feeling a little unseemly.

All that tensed muscle seemed to melt, but he still looked away, his face low. "That uh, that hasn't happened before— I'm sorry, I—"

The brush of her fingers across his softening hard-on cut him off. "It's okay."

Dean's eyes flicked back to her, searching her face.

"We'll just have to be careful next time." Robin almost told him he should go down on her later, but saying that aloud felt even more extreme than she'd behaved tonight. "Just not tonight." Without being swept along in the moment she could think and now felt vulnerable here at the office, but she didn't want to go anywhere else either. Like a splash of cold water the little interruption had popped the tension in the room and Robin had lost her mood for sex. They had to do this right, like normal people with actual dating instead of her throwing her legs around him at the first opportunity.

Dean paused, his breath coming careful. "So that mean there'll...be a next time?"

Robin licked her lips. "Well I mean, that's if you want there to be." The confidence that had so easily filled her now drained through her feet.

Wrapping his arms around her and squeezing tight, Dean leaned in and nuzzled her maw, nibbling at the fur along her jaw. "I do," he whispered. "I hope you do too."

He really wanted to be with her, he liked her. This had been hot. Whatever happened, Robin allowed herself to believe this had been the right thing to do, and things were going to be okay.

"As long as I don't have to wear this stupid freaking costume again."

Dean laughed against her throat, and Robin joined him.

STRANGE ON A TRAIN

When this was all through, Marjani would lovingly murder her little sister.

It was Nyala's fault she rode on this miserable excuse for a train. All of the seats designed for larger species were taken despite the car only being a fifth of the way full. Despite having the fairly lithe and flexible physique of a serval, she somehow could not find a comfortable position no matter how she tried—and oh, how she had tried. Marjani thought ahead to bring a blanket, but assumed it would be so easy to sleep on the train she'd not seen a need to bring a pillow, and scoffed when the train offered a kit with a pillow for eight dollars. Now she would have paid twice that, but the overpriced food car where they sold it had closed for the night three hours ago. Marjani already tried curling up and using her rolled-up blanket as a pillow, but a piece of the seat jabbing into her hip ruined the position she slept in best. The position going the other way put her closed eyes in line with the central light going down the car's center, and while it lacked intensity, her feline night vision turned it into a beacon.

Tying it all together, some big species like a horse was filling the car with an awful noise—calling it snoring would have been an insult to those who snored, as the individual birthed a sound more like a duck being run through a dilapidated diesel engine. Damn her large ears. At home, any persistent noise had to be hunted down and silenced before she could relax, so of course she wound up in the car with the one individual that left her aching to take her claws to either her ears or his neck.

Oh yes, so much murder.

Of course, Marjani had agreed in advance to help her sister for the first month after she gave birth. Then, managing to ruin plans like she somehow always did, Nyala had to go into labor a week early. Bad weather at the connecting airport meant there had been no way Marjani could reschedule her ticket. She would have the credit towards another ticket of equal price in the future, but that didn't help her now. Of course, the train between here and there meant a ten-hour trip.

She plotted a little revenge upon her mother, too. "Don't drive," her mother had insisted. "You on the road make me worry, too! Can't you just get on a train? See the countryside. Romantic!"

Romantic? That really dug the claws in, too. The whole mess had forced Marjani to miss her anniversary with Amadi. She always anticipated the event, a day they had set aside each year to be more wild than their usual, but fulfilling, sex lives.

Maybe the cat wouldn't be so tightly wound if there had been good sex before the trip. Of course, there hadn't been time.

Well no sense scratching for sleep that wouldn't come. With a growl she sat up, only to find a flock of stray hairs in her eyes, released from its simple bun by her constant repositioning. She brushed it aside and marveled at the mess of it; back in high school, a boy had written her a poem where he called her hair "a beach at twilight"—she had really loved that, back then—but beneath this lighting it brought to mind dirty clay. Marjani tried arranging it into something manageable for the next few hours.

She climbed from her seat and, leaving her shoes behind, prowled down the aisle towards the bathrooms. Not needing to go, the serval instead took a few moments to touch her toes, squat, lift each leg as high as she could, then curl them. Her tail received a flicking, stretching workout too. Beneath her the train bucked and rolled along its path and she swayed to keep her balance, once needing to catch herself on the wall. If she got off the train during their fifteen minute delays at the one or two stops along the route then she could have walked around amid the smokers, but a little fear of being left behind kept her on the train. At least the seats had enough leg room—much of Marjani's height came from the long, sleek legs of a serval, ones a boyfriend had remarked "went up to her neck."

Someone coughed behind her. Marjani started and whirled.

A male skunk stood there. A good looking male skunk. Probably still in his twenties, which would put him at least five years younger than her. He was fit in that not-too-much muscle way that spoke of some weights and cardio or lots of swimming. She would've said military but he lacked the bearing, too relaxed and dressed in casual clothing that still managed to make him look good. Maybe volunteer firefighter or police?

"Could you move back a little, please?"

Marjani's eyes flicked to her sides. Of course she was blocking both bathroom doors. "I'm so sorry," she said and scooted back.

"It's okay," he said, voice heavy and worn out. Now she noticed his fur mussed and sticking out, and his saggy, haggard stare.

She let the exhaustion creep into her own voice. "Can't sleep either?"

"Nope." After returning the tired smile he disappeared into the bathroom with a ca-chunk of the lock, leaving his scent behind.

The serval slinked back to her seat.

When she first climbed aboard Marjani had chosen a seat behind and opposite a skunk, thinking no one else would want to. Sure enough, three empty rows in either direction from the skunk, aside from her own. That had probably been him. Standing up and peering over to find a skunk-less seat confirmed it. While some of the more olfactorily-sensitive species kept well clear, her dull feline nose wasn't so offended, especially given she'd gotten used to it as a kid while playing house and wedding and space-princesses with the skunk two doors down.

Well, if she wasn't getting any sleep then she needed some distraction. Marjani leaned back and tried to get comfortable, sliding her tail through the hole in the seat's back and into the tail-pouch. A perk of having a shorter tail meant she had more room to flick it. She popped in her headphones, started an audio book, and tried to relax. Of course breathing in to calm her nerves just reminded her again of this miserable train; whatever filters they used to clear the air of mixed-species smells must have been broken, as the collective scent of the passengers, both past and present, had become potent. At least she wasn't canine.

Focusing on the story unraveling in her ears took the rest of the distractions away. Ever since she had been little, listening to things and talking was more enjoyable than watching or reading them—maybe it was having tall ears for a cat? Did rabbits prefer audio or the sound of a conversation to more visual things? The audio book kept her attention for the next hour.

Until the book slid into a sex scene.

So wrapped up in the story, Marjani rode along with the

characters, feeling the anticipation, the excitement—until she found herself turned on. Of course. No, she didn't need arousal on top of everything right now, but if she paused it there would be little else to do, and she wanted to finish this scene anyhow. She let it play on. By the time it ended Marjani's nipples ached with stiffness.

Of course, a new layer of torture for this trip. She sat, squirming, longing for their anniversary games even more now. Too bad she couldn't take care of this and relieve some of her stress.

...Why couldn't she?

The thought caressed its way deep into her mind. It was nearly 3 AM—who would notice?

Discreet public sex had never been something she could convinced Amadi to try. Too much of a risk of getting caught, he'd said, but since the poor man had trouble using a crowded public restroom, Marjani suspected performance anxiety had something to do with it. For her the potential risk didn't bring the thrill; what excited her was *getting away* with it.

How could she get away with it?

Going to the bathroom to take care of this was out of the question—they had the appeal of an airplane toilet with just a little more leg room. Terrible mood killer.

What about her smell? Always her chief concern for getting away with public endeavors. Would it drift far? No, with the scent filters not doing their job, any arousal wouldn't make a dent in the blanket of concentrated aromas that had settled over the car. The seats around her were vacant too, on account of the skunk, so another favorable point.

She only needed to be alert for the occasional passenger headed to the bathroom. Easy enough, right?

Sadly, no toys—she wouldn't be digging the travel vibe from one of her suitcases stowed above—so this had to be done the old fashioned way.

First Marjani collected some paper towels from the bathroom and spread them over her seat.

Hiking her loose travel skirt, the serval sat down on the papers and slid her underwear down. The blanket went over her lap. Perfect, no one could see anything. As a final touch she slid an earbud in and set her player to a bundle of quick erotic stories, just the thing to guide her fantasies. She had made preparations for a little self-care at her sister's house— a *lot* of stress helping with newborn cubs and a moody new mom would need relieving—but a little head start couldn't hurt.

With one eye half-open and an ear swiveled towards the aisle, Marjani glided fingerpads over her folds. She caressed at first, but soon fingers were in knuckle deep, casting aside any pretense of going slow. Needing more room to move and be comfortable, she draped her leg across the other seat, spreading herself wide beneath the blanket and, with the new freedom, put some aggression into her wrist's rolling.

The short, steamy stories rolled by, dragging her deeper into the fantasy. Her purring had built up by the time she reached up to squeeze her breast and play with the aching nipple. Not close, but definitely on the fast track there. When she finally put thumb to clit, she let out a low moaning mewl.

Marjani sucked air through her teeth, eyes springing open, and she went still. Did anyone hear that? Had she made noises she hadn't noticed?

Of course she'd forgotten the noise! Amadi had always encouraged her be to be vocal; privacy hadn't been an issue since college, except on holidays when they wanted to sneak in some intimacy while staying with relatives.

Holding her breath—which vibrated in a weird, ticklish way when she purred—she looked around and strained her ears. Nothing looked different, it-

Marjani made eye contact with her voyeur.

Across the aisle, the far seat in the row ahead leaned back while the seat next to it stayed upright, allowing the skunk to peek back at her with a keen grey eye.

The heat boiling between her legs and beneath her fur lanced right up to her ears and she snapped her legs closed, the motion squashing the blanket and baring a long line of thigh. Her eyes squeezed closed and she breathed hard. Of course she had been caught.

Even through the embarrassment a steamy thought seeped through her body. He had been watching her. Why did that turn her on so much? Was it just because she was already aroused, or…? Either way, why stop?

The skunk had looked away, maybe because he'd been caught or she'd stopped. Still turning the question over in her mind, Marjani couldn't find a reason why she should stop. Eventually she opened her legs again and began anew, slower this time despite her burning need. This time though she turned her audio book off—the cat had enough to fantasize about.

Like that hunky skunk. How big was he? How would it feel with him on top of her? Dwelling on that, she decided there was no harm in letting him see a little bit more. She even gave him a name in her mind: Hunk.

Marjani nudged the blanket off her legs and eased out a moan on the same octave as a snore. As she watched the skunk's head turned, and this time she caught his eye, grinning while she made a show of rolling her wrist with her pumping. At this angle Hunk probably couldn't see the good details, so for him one of her hands came up to squeeze her breast and toy with the nipple, her eyes sank to half-mast and her mouth curled into an "o".

Of course it was that moment someone walked past on the way to the bathroom.

Frozen in place, her heart and breath didn't start working

again until she heard the ca-chunk of the bathroom lock. Then she could relax. Someone walking to the bathroom isn't focusing too keenly on the seats on either side of them, as with every step their eyes move along. All they would recognize was "cat, sitting up," without staying long enough to pick up the finer details, especially in this lighting.

Still, she had to pay a little bit more attention to her surroundings. After a renewed smile at her watcher, the serval arched her back and returned to the task beneath her touch, filling herself with two digits and imagining they were his dick.

Marjani could fuck him.

The thought startled her enough to give her pause, but she renewed her efforts as the notion unfurled, this time keeping her fires stoked instead of chasing an orgasm.

On their fifth anniversary, she and Amadi had swapped with another couple. Since then they had established a little arrangement: a third partner was acceptable if they both talked about it, agreed on it, and it happened only once with that partner. Both of them had enjoyed two others apiece. Almost always the spouse out of the action watched—more out of precaution than voyeurism—except that one time schedules couldn't mesh.

Enjoying this stranger here and now bent the rules, but she could.

She reached for her cellphone while keeping her digits busy. A call would wake poor Amadi on a work night but she wanted the peace of mind. Of course she had no bars. Miserable, shitty train.

The best she could do was to send a text. "There's a guy on the train that I'm going to try to have sex with. I'll keep you posted." It likely wouldn't get sent until she was somewhere with decent cell reception, but it was a start.

Marjani would need to make it up to Amadi. Make it up

well.

It was all moot if Hunk didn't bite. Getting him would be tricky too. A female being assertive and making a bold first move would throw a good number of guys right off their "game," so she had to bring him to her.

After waiting for the elderly rabbit to leave the bathroom and return to her seat, Marjani turned her body towards the skunk and opened her legs. While stroking herself, she propped her ankle on the seat's armrest, her underwear dangling right off the end of her foot. That foot wiggled back and forth for a moment before flicking her panties into the aisle between the seats. Briefly she wished she'd worn a more impressive pair.

The skunk glanced down, then back to her. Her eyes met his, went down to the panties, then back to him, a pout creeping across her muzzle. Then, flashing a most hungry smile, the serval kissed her thighs together and curled up on her seat, waiting with her tail twitching across the cushion beside her.

Sure enough, he got up. Hunk plucked her underwear off the floor and leaned against the seat in front of her, whispering, "Excuse me, miss…." He extended them. "I think you dropped these?" An intrigued, perhaps excited smile rode along his lips, and she thought she saw Hunk take a deep breath of the aroused scent thick around her. He didn't look too tired any more.

"Oh, thank you," she said and reached out, brushing her wet fingerpads across the back of his hand as she reached for them, then hesitated. "Maybe you can keep them if you help me. My fingers are getting tired and yours look so big and capable…." Keeping her dark eyes wide and pleading, Marjani's smile became canary-eating and she arched her back just so.

He stood up straight and she thought she caught sight of

his tail flipping up in surprise. Hunk glanced around, probably going through the same mental checklist she had, before pocketing her panties and settling into the seat next to her. Earning some points right out of the gate he reached down to cup her inner thigh but stopped there, his eyes on hers.

Marjani tilted her hips towards him, widened her legs and held eye contact.

He started out coy. Tracing her folds, ringing her clit. Any other time she'd have welcomed the slow build, but Marjani's engine was well and truly revved.

Glancing down, she was going to direct his hand to be more vigorous when his watch caught her eye. Not just expensive but it had two sets of numbers: the traditional hours in an inner ring, and an outer ring of increments of five leading up to 60. A diving watch. A coworker had gone on and on about it before her vacation to the islands. Hunk became a surfer for her—no, a diving instructor, swimming among tropical reefs in a tight scuba suit.

The skunk brought her back to reality by cupping her mound and grinding his palm into her. "Yes," she hissed, lifting her hips to push against his touch. Exactly what she needed. Hunk grinned, rubbing in a tight circle before drawing it back to sink two digits inside of her. Now she squeezed his hand with her thighs and tucked her face into his shoulder to groan.

Being this close to Hunk's scent overloaded Marjani's nose and her eyes began to water. A skunk's base aroma didn't stink on its own so much as overwhelm from the sheer strength of it, like a concert's volume could leave someone temporarily deaf. She would adjust, but at first the serval sat stunned, occasionally twitching from his strumming fingers.

When she could finally pay attention, she noticed Hunk's tail draped over both of their laps. The big, broad brush probably couldn't fit in the seat's tail pouch. A welcome perk that gave Marjani cover to grab him by his hard-on and squeeze before reaching for his belt. The skunk found her clit and polished it with his thumb, freezing her in place. Her eyes squeezed closed as her insides shuddered, leaving her fumbling at his pants dumbly.

Special care had to be taken for her to not tear her claws through his pants while unfastening. Finally the serval wrapped her fingers around Hunk's cock and put that enthusiasm into her pumping, working him with enough speed and intensity to earn a nice fap noise. Larger than Amadi by an inch and a little thicker. Hunk had more than enough to satisfy. Marjani wanted him inside her, but needed to hold off for now.

Focusing on his smell helped her slow down. Normally opening anyone's pants meant being hit with a lustful aroma, but his natural odor hung over the sexier smell; if she had walked by him after he'd fucked, there's a good chance she wouldn't notice, and, even this close to his cock, she was just now able to pick it up. But if she fucked him, there would be no way to get rid of the harsh scent without a shower. A price worth paying.

Slowing her strokes, the serval ran her fingerpads along the crown, then curled one digit to tickle the sensitive tip with her fur, making him jump. She chuckled and looped a single finger around the ridge just under his head and tugged.

"I like your big dick," she purred into his ear. "Would you like to fuck me with it?

"Yeah," he grunted and tried to thrust into her hand. The serval let him, wrapping her fingers around him again, squeezing as he bucked.

"Mm, it's too bad we don't have any lube. I love taking it in my ass." She didn't, but he didn't need to know that. From the way Hunk leaned closer and put his shoulder into his fingering, it certainly made an impression. She groaned again,

35

once more too loud, and clenched down on his fingers, then softer around his shaft.

"Want me to go down on you?"

Her eyes flicked down to the floor. The train seats had more leg room than a plane, and while he'd be cramped, Hunk could definitely fit down there on his knees.

Marjani glanced back to meet his grey eyes. "You are my hero."

Grinning all the while, Hunk knelt and curled into place. After draping a leg over his shoulder, she covered him and her lap with the blanket. It couldn't hide his tail, the striped brush stuck out beside him and curled under the seat, hidden from notice.

The serval's hips jerked with his first lick. The second stroke, one long swirl that ended inside her, left her gasping. On the third pass he found her clit and Marjani had to cup her mouth to keep from waking the car. Tightening her leg over his shoulder pulled his face right into her mound and she shoved herself against his nose. Hunk put his lips and tongue to work with more gusto, going so far as to push a hand under her raised thigh and grab her butt. With a muffled growl she hugged his face with her thighs. Did he do this with all those otter girls he swam with, going down on them on sandy beaches or in sailboats?

A finger teasing her back door brought Marjani out of the fantasy. It only took a nudge with a claw to discourage him.

Hunk kissed her clit, surrounding and squeezing it with his lips. The yowl started in her throat but launched into a muffled squeal as he started to suck. When his tongue and a finger inside her joind the party, Marjani came hard. Don't be loud. Don't be loud. She locked her teeth shut, tucked her nose into the crook of her elbow, and hoped for the best.

Coming down left her nuzzling the seat with a purr revving in her chest. Hunk gave her a few passing caresses through her fur and a farewell lick or two before she let him up, and she could see the dampness of his muzzle. She licked at the mess in between nosings and the stray nip.

"Like that?" he said with an edge of well-justified smugness.

She reclaimed his erection, giving it a squeeze. "Oh yes. Let me thank you for your kindness."

Marjani leaned down and pressed the flat of her tongue along the tip—then pulled back. Like his smell, Hunk tasted dense and powerful, and she took small passes to get used to it. Once adjusted, she ran the flat of her tongue against the head and brushed. Her smooth barbell piercing provided a nice contrast to her tongue's roughness—something she knew since Amadi had the same piercing, a mutual experiment they tried and kept. She paid particular attention to the ridge along his glans. For several moments she toyed with Hunk's shaft, batting his crown while keeping her hand stroking smoothly

He wanted more. It was obvious in his frustrated breath, how he pushed against her mouth to try and get her to take it in, his thigh tensing as he held back from thrusting into her face. Finally he gripped the back of her neck and grunted, "Suck it."

Poor Hunk, teased so cruelly. At least she earned some dirty talk in return.

"Sorry stud," she said and sat up. "I only wanted a taste. What I really need is this inside me." The pump of her hand increased before she squeezed the tip.

Hunk groaned and said, "How are we going to do this?"

Marjani thought for a moment. They could sit on their sides facing one another, and she then throw a leg over his hip? Too slow and intimate for what she wanted with a stranger, and more importantly it had zero room for discretion. Riding him worked but, while lovely in these seats, would again be too obvious.

Standing up—ow dammit, she hit her head on the low luggage overhang—she first stepped into the aisle and looked around. So far no one seemed to have noticed. The serval first fiddled with her suitcase in the overhang, just to look normal in case someone looked, then she grabbed her skirt and stepped back in, hiking it up as she settled on Hunk's lap facing away.

"Before we start, you're loud." Hunk reached into his pocket and pulled out her underwear. "I think you could use a gag."

Probably six out of ten women would have been upset or grossed out by the suggestion, but Marjani's eyes flashed in wicked approval, her mouth opened and she took them. Her teeth would shred them before long and she didn't care one bit.

She lifted up and scooted back, hovering as the skunk brushed himself against her folds. Instead of lining up though, Hunk swirled his glans around, teasing her some more. A glare over her shoulder made him chuckle, but he stopped and slotted himself in.

Digging her claws into the seat in front of her, Marjani eased back on him.

The gag worked. She moaned into it as he started to fill her, and she picked up the hitch of his breath once most of him sank in. When her butt settled on his lap, she wiggled and leaned back, basking in the feeling of being full. Yes, this was exactly what the serval needed. Breath fluffed the fur of her nape before Hunk nibbled at her scruff, making her insides clench around him, and she arched into the hand cupping her breast.

Marjani started to rock, testing both the noise of the seat and how best to move in the position. The seat complained, but no louder than the train's natural racket. While nice, the rocking just wasn't doing it for either of them. Hunk pushed against her harder than necessary and she didn't blame him.

They struggled to find a good way to give her leverage, finally ending up with Hunk's hands bracing her back while she clung to the seat ahead of her. Marjani tightened her thighs, arched her back against his hands, and started to bounce. Soon she built up a heavy locomotion, her butt slapping his pelvis with a muffled whump. When he added his own bucking to the mix, she moaned through the gag.

On the way down she paused, leaning back into his supportive hands. Taking her sopping makeshift-gag out, Marjani panted over her shoulder, "Warn me before you come."

Hunk grunted, "Okay," and kept his starving upward thrusts.

The serval waited until she had eye contact before putting the underwear back in, then dropped her hand between their legs and cupped his balls. He squeaked through his nostrils and shuddered. Holding tight to the seat in front of her and leaning back against his bracing hands, she sashayed her hips sideways, swirling on his shaft and rhythmically clenching it.

The train chose that moment to tilt subtly on the track as it often did, and she nearly toppled into the floor.

He nudged her thigh with a hand and patted beside his own. "Bring your legs up, put your knee here."

Duh, why hadn't she thought of that? Marjani lifted one leg at a time until her shins pressed into the seat on either side of Hunk's legs and gave an experimental few bounces. Now with better support and able to work her legs, she felt far more control.

Now with a better grip, Marjani took the moment to tilt her head out into the aisle. No one looked like they were paying attention. She would spot anyone moving towards her, but she was blind to anyone coming up behind them, and they'd definitely see her ears and the top of her head steadily bobbing.

Hunk gripped her shoulders and yanked her down. She yowled, the gag only blunting it, and her heart leaped across her tongue. They both stilled, but only for a breath or two before Hunk nudged her forward and Marjani snatched the seat again.

If that's how he wanted it then she would deliver. She dug herself in, leaned forward, and put her back into riding. Instead of just dropping back, Marjani shoved against the seat in front of her, slamming her ass into him and grinding.

Her breath pumped out of her in a raspy whine, and even her muscles started to ache. Easing into a more manageable bucking, she dropped a hand down between her thighs and abused her clit, tossing finesse to the wayside. Marjani was close, blissfully close, the pressure struggling below her bellybutton like a boiler readying to burst.

Through the climbing tension, Marjani's sharp ears caught the whoosh-shunk of a door at the end of the car opening. Shit. She jerked her head to peer out into the aisle—nearly toppling off the skunk's lap onto her face—and spotted a train employee beginning down the aisle. Shit shit shit.

Hunk helped pull her back into his lap, but she grabbed his arms, hugged them against her and dropped sideways into the seat beside them. Marjani curled partially into a ball and Hunk halfway spooning her. The skunk settled in behind her more smoothly, and thankfully he got the message, his tail curling around their waist and kept still.

Both held their breath.

The serval's ears swiveled to track the train employee approach, then pass by them without pause.

A hundred tense heartbeats later and the door at the back of the car opened. Hunk let his breath out on her nape and, because he was already spooning her, it was so easy to slide into her and start thrusting. Had she not been gagged, ready to come, and close to panic, she'd have laughed or slapped him playfully. Instead the serval opened her legs and resumed working her clit, frantic to get off before some other interruption leapt into their laps.

The climax crashed into her, flushed through her, leaving her fur on end. The serval pressed her face into her seat and let a scream loose into the cushion.

Her insides still danced the samba when she picked up on the skunk's urgency.

He hissed, "Getting close."

With still-wobbly legs, Marjani uncoiled and stood up, the motion dislodging Hunk with a squeaking growl of dismay. She planted one knee in the seat, pressed her upper body against the window until the cool glass bit her nipples, and hiked her hips towards him. An arched tail and a glance over her shoulder finished the deal. She could scream "Fuck me" without a sound.

Hunk mounted her and plunged inside like he was on fire and needed to beat the flames out against her body. The skunk pounded against her without finesse or rhythm, but after all the teasing and position-juggling, she didn't fucking care. Her face wound up pressed to the cool glass, fogging it with every breath.

A third delicious climax was on the horizon when he burst inside of her. Hunk pushed in deep and kept pushing, his hips thrashing sideways, and he held on tight as if he might fall off or fly apart. Looking back over her shoulder, she could see the tightness in his features and his big, striped tail flailed about in the aisle like a wind-caught sheet. The only sound in the whole affair was a single, deep and prolonged grunt that trailed off into an, "Ahh."

Hunk finally sagged against her, gasping into her neck, and she pulled the ruined underwear out of her mouth so she could pant, too.

A thought shined in her eyes. Marjani leaned sideways, reaching down into her purse, and took out her phone. Flicking the screen until she found the right function, the serval nudged Hunk and passed him the phone. "Lean back, take my picture."

"Wha?"

"To remember this by," she purred.

Hunk snapped a picture or two before she nudged him with her elbow. "Pull out," she urged and when he did, the serval cupped her ass cheek, pulling it open as she parted her thighs wider. "Get a good shot of the mess." Amadi would love this.

Grinning over her shoulder, she watched Hunk's lust-awed expression while the flash popped off.

That was how she saw orange lights of a station settle in the window behind him. The train came to a stop with a slight lurch and a squeak. The lights barely brightened and a soft voice murmured from the PA system, "Hamilton, fifteen minutes." All through the car people woke and stirred all around them, and the door at the far end opened.

Of course.

MISSED

The click-clack of Miss Pendigrass's riding boots echoed down the hall in her wake, the sound helping to transform her walk from a stately stroll to the confident, no-nonsense prowl more suited to an executive. She passed a hall monitor, and instead of her customary smile and greeting, she snapped her muzzle up at a curt, acknowledging angle. The motion forced her to nudge her slender glasses back into place.

The border collie quieted her heels as she neared her destination. From her purse she removed a tiny black remote, adjusted the dial to two, and glanced into the window in the closed door.

Beth moved among the rows of desks, passing out papers and instructions.

Miss Pendigrass aimed the remote and fired.

The mink's body jerked, her back and tail going straight, and Miss Pendigrass could almost hear Beth's sharp intake of breath. The border collie lingered long enough to catch sight of momentarily wide eyes, tail fur puffing out, and a roll of the hips so subtle one would have needed to be looking to spot it.

Before she was spotted at the door, Miss Pendigrass renewed the cadence of her boots. She was certain Beth should have composed herself by the time the border collie reached the end of the hall. Even though the activation times were random, the mink had ample time to become accustomed to wearing the bullet vibe over the last several Wednesdays. A shame the vibrations had only a five minute lifespan when the remote was beyond range.

This time she was not merely keeping the girl on her toes.

Every step and breath added to the building anticipation and power, growing for the coming meeting. It had become overwhelming now, the imaginary pressure like a preheating oven, hot and trembling in her chest. The sensations had begun to snowball an hour ago when she received the email.

"Miss, I very much need to see you at lunch. It's important."

Tracing her steps back out of Parker Hall and up the library steps, Miss Pendigrass strode towards the central desk. "Meredith," she called, "I'm taking a lunch."

The aged lynx's tufted ears turned Miss Pendigrass's way before the rest of her.

It was difficult to put away the mood she had been cultivating, set aside with a deep breath before she snapped at Meredith. The border collie spared her colleague a smile, tapped her own watch, then mimed putting something into her own mouth.

"Ah! I'll hold down the fort," Meredith said, reaching for the volume on her hearing aid.

By the time she opened the library door, Miss Pendigrass was once more enveloped in her headspace. She walked around the building until she reached the fire door and unlocked it from the outside. The stairwell beyond took her three flights, leaving her panting by the end, and she pushed into the cramped corridor beyond. She passed ancient cobwebs and dust motes dancing in the slim bars of sunlight slipping through a high grimy window. At the far end of the hall, she opened the store room and stepped inside.

The air and floor were less dusty here than it should have been, and the clutter was minimal, providing a full space to maneuver around the central table, lit by the feeble efforts of a single naked light bulb. It was a meager set, but it was Miss Pendigrass's stage. At the far end of the room she moved aside two boxes of old yearbooks before hoisting up the third. After setting the box down on the table, she peeled her sweater over her head and folded it.

The email had said it was important. Miss Pendigrass imagined it was; Beth had not been directed to climax in nine days. The mink must have been on fire.

Beth's class must certainly be out by now.

Her nipples were tight beneath the lace of her bra, and a familiar warmth tensed below her waistband. Miss Pendigrass removed her bra, leaving her considerable bosom to sag, and folded her bra atop her sweater. From inside the box she took her first prop, a dark purple bustier, pulling it into place.

Beth must be on her way.

The thought set the border collie's tail to wagging. This meeting was important for them both. Their engagements so far had been limited to the exchange of power and the physical. Now Miss Pendigrass felt ready to close the roles between them. She would take this beyond games, she would take the girl home and relax her heart.

The border collie lost her trousers and underwear, replacing them with a dark, sheer lace skirt shorter than the boys wished the girls could wear their uniforms. Miss Pendigrass left her riding boots on. Then she removed a few props from the box and her purse, arranging them on the table.

When she heard the fire escape door open at the end of the hall, Miss Pendigrass took two of her props in hand and poised by the door.

Four knocks echoed through the heavy door, in a one-two-one pattern. Miss Pendigrass smiled. "Come in."

Beth pushed the door open. The poor lighting turned her mahogany fur and dark hair smoky against the pearl blouse with its brass buttons. Just the sight of her left Miss Pendigrass wanting to touch her, hold her, nuzzle her throat and breathe in that wonderful wildflower scent that she loved so much. She wanted her linens to smell like Beth.

Beth lifted timid brown eyes up to the librarian. As soon as Miss Pendigrass caught her gaze, she extended her riding crop. A red ribbon choker dangled off the end.

Beth took a breath, color creeping into her ears. "Miss," she said. "I need to…"

When Miss Pendigrass hardened her stare, the girl dropped her eyes and had barely formed a syllable before the border collie brought the choker into her field of vision.

For a moment she darted eyes up to Miss Pendigrass before glancing to the choker, then she plucked it off the crop and fastened it in place.

"Good. Now, strip to your panties."

"Yes Ma'am," Beth said. "Miss, could you please not use the toy when I'm standing in full view? I was handing bac-!" She spasmed, nearly tearing a button.

Miss Pendigrass set the dial to four before returning the remote to the table. "You're wearing my collar right now, girl. What does that mean?"

Beth shuddered and ducked her head, voice both chastised and stimulated.

"Th-that I am to follow all rules."

"Yes, and what is the rule about talking?"

"Only when spoken to," Beth said.

"And what time have we set aside for discussions for both playtime and other matters?"

Beth's digits dug into her blouse. "During aftercare and in emails, Miss."

"And is now either of those times?"

"No ma'am."

"Then," Miss Pendigrass said, tilting Beth's chin upwards with the end of the crop so that she could stare into the girl's eyes, "undress and come here."

The mink's ears flattened, but she nodded against the

crop. First went her blouse. When she reached for her skirt, the border collie's cleared throat sent her hands back up to remove the red bra, baring her small breasts and their black nipples. The skirt came last. Then she came closer.

Miss Pendigrass stepped aside and gestured at the table with her crop. Beth bent over it with deliberate slowness, tail rippling in restrained excitement. The posture best presented the mink's legs encased in dark stockings. A band wound around one thigh just above a garter, holding the battery to the bullet vibe. Its cord fed into the front of Beth's red boyshorts, where Miss Pendigrass could see dew tinting the cotton.

"Mmm." The border collie trailed her nails through the softness along the back of Beth's thigh, leaving furrows in the short but thick velvet of the mink's pelt. Her touch ran from the tight thigh up to the outer lines of Beth's taut little bottom, then to the underside of a cheek, threatening to delve into her rear's crease. The touch sent the mink's tail into an upward arch. "You've been looking forward to this, haven't you?"

"Yes Miss," Beth said with a quiver in her voice that lifted the border collie's ears.

Miss Pendigrass collected a student's tie from the table and walked around until she stood across from Beth's head. "Wrists, Girl."

The mink extended her arms, the motion just long enough to reach across the table's width. Miss Pendigrass looped the tie over Beth's wrists and slid the knot snug.

"Miss, before we continue, this is rea—"

Lifting Beth's chin with a sudden, tight grip, the librarian regarded her girl with a steely glare. She could not tolerate the insubordination any longer. Had it been so urgent to disrupt their play, the email would have said as much. "If you speak out of turn one more time, I will send you home without an orgasm. Is that what you want?"

"No Miss." The defeat and desperation flashing in her eyes was mirrored in her tone.

Tracing Beth's mouth with her thumb, she added, "I haven't given you permission to climax in some time. Would you like more days to be added to that?"

The mink said nothing, but she didn't need to. Miss Pendigrass could see the hunger in her eyes underneath whatever reluctance had bubbled up all of a sudden.

"Good." Taking Beth's now bound wrists, she pulled her arms straight and hooked the loop of the tie on a thin knob that she had screwed in underneath the table's edge. Returning to the toy box she retrieved what looked like a claw hair clip made of metal. Brushing Beth's hair aside, Miss Pendigrass squeezed the toy's end, opening the steel jaws, and sank the little teeth into Beth's scruff.

The mink arched her back and hissed. It always impressed the librarian how minks weren't subdued by a scruff bite, but instead turned wild. Beth's tail lashed and, as Miss Pendigrass reached for her face, she snapped playfully at the collie's fingers. Miss Pendigrass snatched her by the muzzle, and began stroking her whiskers.

Beth's head jerked, but she held firm. Each whisker received a tickle, leaving the mink wriggling on the table, her eyes squeezed closed before fluttering open.

Miss Pendigrass rested the tips of her nails along Beth's shoulder, dragging their points down the mink's back as she walked around to the girl's rear end. Just before reaching the boyshorts' waistband, she turned her hand over, pressing in and rubbing over the cheek in a tight circle. Beneath her hand the mink shuddered, and Miss Pendigrass noticed her thighs pressed flush together. It was only then that the scent caught her nose, and she blinked.

She pulled her groping hand back while with the other

she pressed the remote's off button.

Immediately tension eased out of Beth's muscles.

Miss Pendigrass snapped her free hand across Beth's rear with a muted *thmp* of palm on furred derriere.

The mink jumped with a squeak. Before she had even settled on the table the other cheek received a slap, drawing out another high noise.

Reaching down, Miss Pendigrass claimed the riding crop once more. "Now," she murmured, running the tip along the outside of Beth's thigh, "should I use the sting?" She then picked up a ruler, mirroring the motion along the opposite leg. "Or the thud?"

"The second, Miss. Please?" Beth glanced over her shoulder and hiked her hips up, giving her bottom a faint wiggle.

Miss Pendigrass set the crop aside. But before settling in, she took up the remote once more, dialed the toy to one, and turned it on. Beth sighed under her breath and arched her back, tail kept well out of the way, and swayed her pelvis.

This saucy waggle earned her ruler slap across an inner thigh. Miss Pendigrass could not contain her wag at the resulting moan that bubbled out of Beth's throat.

The librarian set about her task, each crack of the ruler upon a thigh or buttock drawing out a groan or gasp, the pitch and type varying with the power and placement of each strike. The sweetest notes came from the crease where thigh met buttock, or where the cheek, hip and thigh converged. She played the mink like some erotic musical instrument, performing with a tempo that left them both panting and damp.

Setting aside her ruler and turning the bullet vibe off, she began to first graze Beth's sore spots with her nails, flirting with the aching muscles. When the mink squirmed and twitched her tail, silently begging for more, Miss Pendigrass cupped the girl's abused behind, grinding her palms into the ripe cushions while squeezing in lazy rhythms.

Beth laid her face down and groaned into the table, spreading her legs and pushing back into the massage. Miss Pendigrass could see the saturated nature of Beth's underwear, and the smell was intoxicating. Her fingers pressed into the wet material, bearing down on Beth's mound. "Tell me how much you want release, girl. Tell me."

"I...I..."

"Yes?" Miss Pendigrass growled, pinching the mink through her panties.

Beth squeaked, then took a deep breath and whimpered out, "Sanctuary."

Miss Pendigrass paused, a breath away from peeling Beth's panties down and cocked her head. What did that have to do with what she asked?"

Then significance dawned and she yanked her hands back as if burned. With a tight frown, the border collie first looked over Beth for any problems, having noticed no signs of distress. Circling the table, she quickly unbound Beth's wrists and removed the scruffer. "Are you alright?" Not yet touching the girl, she merely leaned in close.

Beth sat up and rubbed her wrists. Still not looking at Miss Pendigrass, she removed her collar.

"Talk to me," the border collie said, her ears splaying.

"That's what I've been trying to do, Miss. But you haven't let me." The frustration and hurt in Beth's whisper was palpable, enough to droop the librarian's tail.

She had yet to look up. Miss Pendigrass reached out, brushing the backs of her fingers along Beth's cheek, then down to cup her chin, drawing the girl's eyes up. "I'm listening now."

Once more Beth pulled her head away and, with a shaky breath, said, "There's someone who is trying to...trying to get me to um. Date them."

The bottom dropped out of Miss Pendigrass's libido. "I see." She tried to sound as neutral and comforting as possible, but even to her ears she failed.

The girl curled up on the table and clutched her tail in her lap, stroking the fur. "I wanted to ask permission. If I could pursue it, ma'am." Beth's ears flattened and she spared a glance up.

Miss Pendigrass felt silly in her getup. She walked from the table, tail giving a fitful tick-tock. Arms crossed under her breasts, she asked, "Does this mean that you want to stop what we're doing?"

"No ma'am," Beth said, quick and loud. "I love these times."

"Then have you told her about our arrangement?"

Once more the mink's voice was tiny. "He, Miss. He."

Her stomach flipped. Miss Pendigrass turned on her. "He? You told me you weren't interested in males. That you had never—"

"I'm not! I wasn't!" Ears pinkening and nose buried in her tail, the mink shook her head. "I've never been, before. But Conner's…sweet. So very sweet and polite, he swims, and he's so good with kids, loves them like we do. He doesn't make me feel like the way I feel around most males, but the way that I am with you, and with the girls before you."

"What is he? His species." She asked something irrelevant to try and rein in her own feelings, but the words cracked once. Be calm. Swallow it for now.

"Dog. I mean, a golden retriever."

Inside, the border collie snorted. Why did women fawn all over those godforsaken knots? Through her quiet scorn, she noticed wetness glistening at the corners of Beth's eyes, and the way she curled up even further, clutching her tail.

The welling tears melted the border collie just a hint. She padded over and dabbed at the poor mink's eyes with a digit.

Beth hugged her tight, nose pressed into the dog's. "Shh." Miss Pendigrass took a deep breath and swallowed down her wants. "It's alright." It wasn't, but she still stroked the mink's back.

Leaning back, Beth's eyes met Miss Pendigrass's. "I don't want to stop," she whispered.

That drew a smile, but the border collie's tone was firm. "You didn't answer me. Have you told him about our arrangement?"

Beth squeaked. "No!" Redness crept up into her ears. "I don't think he would get it." She flailed her hands quickly, trying to halt response. "The...the..." Beth picked up the crop, wagging it. "I think he's very...sheltered."

"I see." Miss Pendigrass slid off the table, opting to stare at the wall. "Why would you even want a relationship with someone vanilla?" She had tried that. Her unsatisfied needs had became a wedge that had widened problems until it all came crashing down.

"I don't know Miss," Beth said. "Am I not allowed to try?"

After a moment's deliberation, the collie sentenced Beth. "You are going to tell him."

Beth shook her head. "I will but not unless things moved towards serious. I don't know if this will work out. Don't you have anyone else you do...this with?"

Instead of saying no, Miss Pendigrass said, "None I'm pursuing a relationship with."

"But Miss! I—"

"Because not only would it be not fair to him," The border collie continued, "not only would some of my existing orders interfere with the potential relationship, but he needs to be put on the same page. If this arrangement is going to work, then we all must talk it out."

Beth gasped. "You want to meet him?"

She did not, but she was going to have to. She had given

her judgment. "Yes."

Ears now scarlet, the mink stared back at Miss Pendigrass with wide eyes.

Miss Pendigrass stared down her muzzle at the girl from her full height and then some. "If it's going to work at all, then everything must be out in the open and clear," she said, giving her edict with a tone of finality.

"I'm very…it's embarrassing," Beth said to her lap. "And Conner's just interested, we aren't dating yet. You're asking me to take all this info and present it like a hiked tail. What if he thinks we're weird or I'm some kind of sex addict or—"

The crack of the ruler across the table caused the girl to jump and snap her head up.

"Enough. Consider it an order," Miss Pendigrass said. "You have permission to pursue the relationship. As long as we outline to him our relationship, and the type of things that excites you. Set a time aside with him, the next time you get the chance, and we'll all sit down. Understood?"

For several moments the mink trembled on the table, but she finally gave a meek nod. "Yes Miss."

"And I'm going to change one of our standing orders, just a little bit." Miss Pendigrass ran the ruler along Beth's thigh while regarding the mink with a rekindling smile. "Instead of keeping your climax all to myself, you're going to start orgasming a lot. Every night at nine fifteen, you're going to start pleasuring yourself. You still can't get off without my permission, so I will expect a phone call when you're close. Understood?"

Once more the mink nodded, her ears still quite glowing, but a faint smile perked. "Yes Miss."

"Once we sort things out with your male, then we can see about adjusting rules to suit everyone. For now, get dressed."

Beth started to slide off the table, then paused. "Miss?"

"Yes?"

"May I…remove the toy?"

Miss Pendigrass smiled weakly. "No." She slid in close and pressed herself against the other female, brushing her fingers downwards and into the girl's underwear. Beth squirmed as she caught, then withdrew the bullet vibe, and let it fall into her underwear.

The mink leaned in and kissed Miss Pendigrass, chaste and affectionate. It broke into a hug where Beth lovingly set teeth to the collie's jaw and throat, and Miss Pendigrass licked her muzzle and cheek. "Thank you Miss," she whispered. "For understanding. For being so kind."

"I am your Miss, it's part of what I'm here to do." She nosed between her mink's still warm ears, licking one, and eased away, allowing the girl to dress and spritz a bit of scent duller to mask the lingering arousal aromas. They shared a conspiratorial smile before Beth wiped the bullet off with a kerchief and tucked it into her purse. Then the girl was gone.

It would go all right. Either the boy would reject the situation, or the love triangle would go on, her providing for some of Beth's needs while he provided for others. The border collie would make it work, and their relationship would continue as it had. It would be alright, she told herself.

This Janine told herself as she retired their toys, but as she looked down at the red ribbon choker, all she could do was quietly cry in the room that smelled so wonderfully of them both.

FIREWORKS

"You must be kidding," I said. "I've heard some crazy requests, but—"

My manager's voice remained as crisp as leaves in November. "I never joke about clients." But then she didn't joke much period. "Desiree, are you turning it down?"

I took a deep breath. "No." I couldn't afford to; this was somewhat of a dry season. Certainly my schedule was wide open for the 4th.

"Good," she said, and I could hear her relief. "You're the only one who matched his specifications." She paused. "He's a deer."

I guess a gazelle was close enough to what would do. "Well, we should meet first to get our stories straight. Can you call him and arrange it?"

"Yes. I'll send him to the Redmund. Goodbye."

I shook my head when she hung up. Why had the agency put a wolf on the phone? In my experience, canines were so caught up in body posture—the position of ears and tails, the scent—they had no ear for phone conversation. Maybe it was prejudiced of me, but wolves were the worst with that body language dependency.

Once I got the call-back, I had a few hours to prepare. Shower, hoof and horn shining, makeup, a slinky but respectable chocolate dress and I was on my way. Before going inside, I texted the agency that I had arrived.

The Redmund was where I liked to do these sit-downs. The hotel staff was polite but not vigilant, the bar's always going, and the restaurant did not charge you by the limb. The industrial air conditioning was a plus—even being a warm weather species, this part of the country had a climate that could be abusive in the summer.

At just-past-quitting-time the restaurant was relatively empty, but it could have been a sports stadium and I still would've picked him out. The glass of soda sat untouched on his table and he folded and unfolded the cloth napkin while staring through the tabletop. I strode to his table, the performance of my walk lost as he never looked up. He must have been deep in thought, never hearing the noise of my hooves on the carpet, because when I said his name his startled jerk nearly took the table with it.

I only smiled, touched the chair across from him and said, "Jacob? I'm Desiree."

"Yes, hi, yes, I'm Jacob, hello," he said all too fast, avoiding eye contact like it might turn him to stone. Then he closed in on himself, arms crossed, head slightly down.

Instead of even bothering to ease into this, I waved the waiter over and ordered myself a glass of wine. It gave him the time to get used to my presence. Although I think he could have used a drink more than I did.

Finally I turned and said, "So Jacob. What is it you do for a living?"

"Software engineer."

I tilted my head, perked my ears and looked impressed. "Really? You must be smart; isn't that complicated?"

"Not really," the deer said and I coaxed him into talking more about the thrilling world of software. As he spoke, and I gave him more attention, he began to loosen up. By the time my wine arrived he actually looked me in the eye.

I continued to probe as I considered him. To say the stag was fat would be unfair; he had a broad frame with what I bet was a sedentary lifestyle, it settled on him like an extra layer of padding. You could see a little thickness along his neck and arms, but his stomach had the most. Plain but not offensively so, dressed in a polo and khakis, and it being the summer he lacked any antlers. Bucks always seemed down or withdrawn at this time of the year, like their racks were physically attached to their pride. While not unattractive he gave the impression of a cuddly and non-threatening friend.

A momentary lull settled when he ran out of things to say, so I set in to finally getting down to business. "So Jacob. Do you know how you want this to go?"

Immediately the wind went out of his sails and he began to fiddle with a napkin. "I…want everyone to believe you're my girlfriend."

"Okay." I reached out and touched his hand, leaning forward and dropping my voice in a comforting tone. "This isn't that unusual. A lot of people hire me to—"

"No," he cut me off, drawing away. "I don't want to pay for that I just—"

"Want someone nice to pose as your girl, that happens a lot," I finished. "Fancy dinners, parties, weddings, once I even posed as a client's fiancée at his high school reunion. I do this a lot. Some males are just so busy professionally they don't have time to find someone, but want others to think they can land an attractive, nice girl. Everyone wants everyone else to think they're successful. There's nothing to be ashamed of here."

I had added that last bit because he still hadn't looked at me, and he started closing up again. It brought his head up and he glanced at me once, but I had the feeling he didn't believe me.

The deer took a deep breath. "I've never brought a girl home, never even told them I've had a girlfriend. I know—*I know* they talk about it, and I don't want them to keep nagging me, keep worrying, keep thinking I'm weird, or a loser, or gay."

"But you're not."

I had said it to be rassuring, but he didn't take it that way. "I'm not gay." He said it quick and with eye contact, but then his voice started to falter. "If I *were* gay I'd bring a guy home just to shut them up."

The laugh snuck out of me. To show it wasn't aimed at him, but with him, I added, "I get a lot of pressure for kids. Do you?"

"Yeah. Well, it eased off some when my brother had a fawn, but it's still there." Jacob let a long sigh through his nose. "I'm just...I don't...talking to women is hard."

"I understand." Reaching out, I pressed my hand over his and smiled again. Oh, I believed him. I understood it. His type: lonely, starved for intimacy and contact. Most males that came to women in my profession were. There was even a term for private encounters with a certain tone, "the girl-friend experience": for the date the professional and client pretended to be in a relationship.

"You're not weird or a loser, Jacob. It's okay." And it was—the last thing clients like Jacob needed was to feel judged, and like a therapist, I had to make him feel comfortable and safe, giving him a place to be himself.

It was smart business. A client who felt good and safe would likely return. "And hey, you're talking to me just fine."

"I guess."

"Are you sure you want to do this?" Part of me hated asking that. If he didn't go through with it, I wouldn't get paid. He'd feel bad about backing out and I'd feel bad about losing a client. But it would be worse if he pulled the plug half way through the date.

The pause that followed had me holding my breath, and when he eked out a "Yes," the stress of my empty bank account relaxed.

He sat up and straightened his shoulders, taking a slow breath. "So," he said with an attempt at a smile, "what uh, what do we do now?"

"Now," I said with a smile, "you tell me about who we need to impress, and then we work out the details of our relationship."

* * *

Two days later I met him in the hotel's parking lot and I got into his car. Normally I'd take my own, but it would be noticed where we were going and look weird coming and going in separate cars if we were together. It was a lengthy trip to the suburbs and it gave me time to test him repeatedly on the ins and outs of our cover story. We couldn't cover all possibilities, so I told him to relax, let me handle most of the questions, ad-lib if something he didn't know came up, and be sure I knew the lie to keep it consistent.

The nervousness eventually eased off, and when the conversation moved to other things, he even relaxed. Jacob grew animated and made wry little jokes once I acted interested in what he had to say. He seemed genuinely nice after he made it over that initial hump and he swallowed his anxiety.

We also dodged the awkward handing over of payment. The hard rule was money up front, but my manager had let me know Jacob paid with a card after our initial meeting. Since we were going to be here several hours but the exact times were uncertain, a full evening charge of $800 settled things. It also meant I was secure the payment was coming, didn't have to worry about carrying or counting it, and my cut was in the mail.

The car pulled up outside of a tawny-colored house that otherwise matched the other cookie-cutter homes in the subdivision. The driveway was so clogged we had to park along the curb behind several other cars. Before we got out I texted the agency to let them know I'd arrived on my date.

Jacob in his cargo shorts and t-shirt led me around the side of the house to the fenced in back yard, where I could already hear voices over the country music and smell the food. With the forecast called for a welcome almost-mild 4th of July, I had went with a butter-cream tank top and a pair of white capris snug enough to emphasize my slender, tight legs and hips while still looking casual.

He looked like he was back to being nervous, but I felt comfortable and ready. I was used to this kind of work; I'm pretty and not gorgeous, not the thing of fantasies, so I get more social than erotic dates (although being a gazelle gave me a touch of the exotic, which drew either kind of client). I had just never heard of something quite like *this*.

He went through the gate first, and because I had to line up behind him, I don't think they saw me at first. I heard a male voice say, "Here comes Jacob, so we must be about ready to eat." When I stepped around him into the yard, a momentary pause settled over the gathered deer. Most were middle aged with a few young faces, all gathered in a knot of lawn chairs or folding chairs, and others seated at two tables pushed together.

"Good," I said loud enough for them to hear me clearly, "I'm hungry."

A brief burst of activity bubbled up with people making comments over one another or sharing pointed looks. That was my cue to get to work.

I strode over to a table off to the side, where a pair of does were uncovering dishes wrapped in saran wrap, and aimed a smile that could light a dark basement at the older of the two, who looked like she was cresting fifty. "Hi," I said, "I'm Rose. You must be Jacob's mother?"

She smiled back, surprise and interest in her eyes. "Hello!

I'm Mary!" Then she glanced at Jacob who had followed behind. "You didn't tell me you were bringing company," she chided him with nervous delight.

"I didn't know I could come until the last minute," I cut in before he replied.

"They're done." We looked over to see a stag of Mary's age carrying over a plate from a still-smoking barbecue. He set it loudly on the table, then noticed me, looked from me to Jacob, and just smiled like he had won something. He wore a shirt with our country's flag blazoned across it. Jacob had told me that the 4th was his father's favorite holiday.

"Oh then it is time to eat. You'll *have* to sit with us," Mary said in a polite way that made it clear we had no room to argue. "It's ready! Everyone, get your plates."

Chairs emptied and everyone gathered in a little line. Like me, they likely had a light breakfast and were waiting for this very thing. Having been here less than two minutes the scent had been getting to me, so I couldn't imagine what those who had been sitting and waiting felt like. I heard conversation, someone saying something to Jacob—and then I saw the spread.

Grilled corn on the cob, Portobello burgers, and kebabs with peppers and cherry tomatoes and other slightly toasted things. Deviled eggs, green beans, potato salad, casserole, macaroni and cheese, and corn bread. Candied yams, banana pudding, cakes and at least one pie I was betting was apple. Being no magician in the kitchen, home cooking that tasted good was rare for me, and a buffet like this was heaven in a plate.

I piled a paper plate full, poured some sweet tea from an icy pitcher, and sat down close to whom I suspected was Jacob's father. Broad like his son but thick with what used to be a laborer's musculature. He also didn't have any food, just a bottle of beer.

"Not going to eat?" I asked before taking a bite of the corn, the buttery kernels bursting and dripping over my chin.

"Mine's coming," he said and smiled. "I'm Luke."

Taking a dip of the tea, I was about to respond before my teeth started to ache from the entire bag of sugar that must have been poured into that tea. Luke laughed, then turned towards the big table. "Mary! We need some of your tea." To me he said, "She'll tell you everyone here except her likes their teeth to rot with every drink."

And she did, when she came over balancing two full plates and a glass of tea, setting one in front of Luke, the other she sat farther down the table in front of a buck who might have just graduated high school, and then gave me my glass. "Thanks," I said to her.

She promised to be right back and went to get her own food. Jacob passed her and sat down next to me. We were certainly getting attention as people filtered back to the tables.

Luke skipped the pleasantries, probably waiting for his wife to eat, and instead immediately launched into a conversation with Jacob over an action movie that had just come out at theaters. While he had told me beforehand, I didn't need the info to see movies were one of the only common grounds they shared.

"Daddy, she has antlers! Why don't you have antlers?" Down the table, a little fawn sat in the lap of a clean-cut, perfect-postured buck. He shot me a smile before shushing her by putting a finger to her lips, which made the little doe pout.

"That's my brother Adam's kid," Jacob said with a smile.

I smelled cigarette smoke before the female deer pushing seventy dropped into a seat at the end of the table, plopping down two beers and her food. It was customary to smoke downwind from everyone else, and she smelled like she had spent the afternoon there. "Hey you brought someone home!" She slapped Jacob on the upper arm. "Way to go!" I had also been warned beforehand about Jacob's grandmother, Charlene.

Mary joined us, saving us from having to reply to that. "So how did you two meet?"

Now I ate with deliberate slowness, both to savor and to draw things out to let me think, even though this had been one of the first things we rehearsed. "My brother. My computer broke, and I called him, thinking he'd know. He didn't, but he plays one of those games that has the many-sided dice with Jacob. Five minutes with Jacob on the phone and he knew what was going on and that it was serious."

"Haha, there you go," Charlene said, leaning over to rub Jacob's shoulder, spilling some of her beer on the ground in the process.

"He's sweet like that," Mary said.

"Yes he is," I said, smiling at him. "He offered to fix it, and when I tried to pay him he said no." Placing my hand on his shoulder, I said, "So I offered dinner and well…"

When he didn't say anything, I nudged him with my knee. "And here we are," he added.

For about five minutes, questions about me dominated the conversation: I was a paralegal. Yes, I liked the city I lived in. I went to the same denomination they did. Why yes I voted for the last President, but of course didn't vote for the current one, and it sure was a shame what he was doing to the country.

A client brought me as a date a few months ago to an event held by a national gun-owners group, raising money for a big "family values" senator. I was in well versed territory here. (Between you and me, a colleague of mine informed me of said senator's interest in diapers and electricity. Shh.)

"Excuse me," I finally said. "'I'm going to get some dessert. Do you want anything?"

Jacob had gone for his second serving while I'd been

chatting, so he shook his head. I felt bad leaving him behind, but I did want dessert, my figure be damned. It just meant more time at the gym later.

I looked up from spooning some banana pudding onto a fresh plate to see Adam sidling up next to me. "So you two are together." His words were direct and precise, a voice used to giving or taking orders. I could tell he was in the military even if I hadn't been briefed.

"Mmhm," I said, moving to the yams.

"You won me twenty dollars."

I looked up. Adam gestured to the young buck that Mary had served earlier. "Paul had money on Jacob being gay."

What wonderful siblings. "Well, if he is gay, then he's a *very* convincing actor," I said with eye contact and suggestive smile to spare. I left him with a stupid look on his face.

As I neared my chair I overheard, "...considered marriage yet?"

Luke frowned. "Mary."

"Oh leave him alone," Charlene said too loudly. "This is his first girl. He probably just wants to break some furniture, sow them wild oats." She laughed and drank, and I suspected that was probably more than her fourth beer.

Luke's disapproving snort came just after a choking noise from Jacob.

"Mother!" Mary scolded. Then, crossly to Luke she added, "I'm his mother. It's my job to worry about these things. It's not as though they'll bring home grandbabies..."

It was then that they all noticed me hovering above my chair. Mary feigned embarrassment while giving me a good hard reading.

I smiled politely and said, "We're still getting to know one another." I sat down and promptly put a fork in my mouth. "These yams are delicious."

Jacob now took the time to get some dessert and all but

bolted from the table.

Charlene leaned over and told me in a too-loud whisper, "Don't think we care that you're not a deer. My second husband was a horse!"

Out of the corner of my eye, I saw Jacob flanked by Adam and Paul. By their grins and the way Jacob's head drooped and was looking at no one, I would have bet they were asking him how well I bounced the bedsprings.

The afternoon went like that. The rest of the gathered had their turn to take a few verbal licks, and a few other personalities brought their own drama that didn't involve either of us.

Finally I turned to Jacob. "Do you think we could make it to my parents' place before the fireworks?"

The relief on his face was priceless. But he said, "Only if I broke some speed limits."

Mary frowned. "You're not going to stay for the fireworks?"

"You gotta come to the bar with me afterwards," Charlene said. She had sobered up—barely.

This I had prepared for. "Sorry. I take some medication that doesn't go well with alcohol."

"It's a karaoke bar!" Charlene cheered. "You can watch the drunks sing!"

"That's okay. I should at least say hello to my mother," I said, as Jacob all but dragged me from the yard.

I knew he was unhappy without looking at him, and his discord was nearly a physical thing when our eyes met over the car before we climbed in. He hired me hoping I would relieve all that pressure and negative attention, and all it earned him was the next level of uncomfortable questions.

No wonder long stretches of interstate separated them. Though I was naturally sympathetic, what with not being on rosy terms with my own family.

Defeat hung like humidity in the car. The silence and tension coming off of him weighed down on me and it sat wrong in my stomach. It happens sometimes, a client not getting what they want because usually either their expectations weren't met or they reacted differently, but a bad date never felt right to me. I should see it as a transaction, but I so far haven't been able to separate that personal element. Especially as with Jacob, I knew how important it was.

Looking out the window, I waited until I saw what I wanted and pointed. "Pull over."

"Huh?"

"Park right over there." I put enough authority in my voice that he didn't question despite the worry on his features.

When the car slid to a stop inside an empty strip mall's parking lot, I unbuckled and turned so I could look at him directly. "Listen, I know this didn't work out how you expected." I placed a hand on his upper arm. "I'm sorry."

He spared me a glance before staring out the window.

Carefully I reached out and touched his muzzle, turning his head to look into my eyes. I could see hurt there. Mostly not from today, but hurt of him over himself. I hated seeing it. Again, I should have been detached.

An escort doesn't just give someone what they want, they strive to give the client what they *need*. I knew what he needed.

I looked into his eyes, leaned close, and said as gentle and earnest as I could, "You didn't ask for this, but I think you deserve it." Leaning in I brushed my lips against his.

Before I could put any more pressure, Jacob pulled back. "I don't want pity." He sounded as wounded as he looked.

"That's not what it's about," I half-lied. You hear that girls in the business don't have sex for money, the sex happens only if they want to—usually that's a lie to cover our ass. Yet it happens, it's happened with me before, and I wanted to now to ease the pain I saw. Maybe that is a little pity there.

Moisture just started to collect at the corners of his eyes, and he looked down and away. A hint of a shake rattled in his voice, one coming from somewhere deep and raw. "You should *want* me."

Leaning in I brushed my nose against his cheek. "What I want is for you to be happy. You are sweet, gentle and smart, and I wish you believed that about yourself."

He tilted his muzzle into the touch. "But I'm not—"

"I want to show you that you are." I nuzzled the top of my muzzle under his. "Will you let me?"

It took so long for him to answer I was about to lean back and buckle up, but then he whispered, "All right."

Cupping his muzzle, I turned his head to me and kissed him again, taking my time now. He replied in kind, hesitating but not completely clumsy with it, and brushed his hand along my neck and shoulder like it might burn him. My lips parted and after several licks along his, we rubbed tongues together at a relaxed pace.

When he warmed up and gained the courage to flirt a finger over my breast, I first pushed against it, then eased back. I caught his eye and pulled my tanktop off, then traced one of my breasts with a finger. "Now your shirt."

A wave of self-consciousness broke over his face. I stroked his muzzle again. "Please?"

It took longer than necessary for him to drag it off and toss it into the back seat with my tank. Again I made eye contact and leaned forward, kissing his chest, brushing my lips over an overweight pec, nibbling daintily just shy of his nipple. His mouth hung agape, nostrils flaring. Skimming my tongue over the little bump of skin in all that fur earned me a throaty noise. I made sure he saw my smile. All the while I slid my fingers along the line of his stomach, barely brushing the fur.

"Nothing here that bothers me, Jacob. I like what I see."

"Really?"

I looked over his round belly and back to his eyes. "Really." In this business you have to swallow any displeasure with the client's appearance because you get all kinds. The same way a waitress smiles and bears it at a rude customer, you have to move on while appearing like you want them. Sure I wasn't melting in my seat but I wasn't put off either. More importantly I cared about him believing me, both as a client and as Jacob.

I rubbed a hand along the top of his thigh, then moved higher. The front of his shorts were quite tense, and already the smell of eager stag started drifting up to me. After drawing down his zipper as slow as I could, I slid a hand inside and cupped his erection, squeezing it and making him twitch in his seat. It felt big and thick like his frame suggested.

For several moments I watched his tightening expression as my hand stroked over him, then popped his button and drew out his cock. The earthy richness of stag's musk flowed up, reminding me of stirred soil and tree bark. I squeezed it and looked around the car.

It would have been less of a hassle to do it here than convince him to drop the money on a hotel room, but it was a poor option. I've only done this a few times in a car, and the limo had been the only remotely comfortable experience. At least Jacob had a spread sedan—a car with more space to accommodate those species with horns or antlers, and those with bulkier frames like horses—so we had more room to maneuver. But I wanted to be in the lead, which narrowed things down to one.

Keeping up the steady stroking I told him, "Lay your seat back." When he had, I relaxed my touches, using just the pads of my fingers to caress first over his length, then under the flare of his crown.

Cradling Jacob's shaft, I leaned forward and grazed my lips along the side of his cock, then up over the head. I toyed with it, kissing around the tip, pressed my lips against it so he felt them open and stretch over him, squeezing and suckling for just a few seconds before dragging off and starting over. I like to look up at partners when I go down on them, but leaning over his lap like this I couldn't. From the snort of his nostrils and a squirm beneath me, I didn't have to wonder that he was enjoying himself. At least he didn't grab hold of my horns—that joke grew old in high school.

I sank down until my nose buried in his sheath, took a deep breath, rocked back up and then down again. Deep throating is a necessary job skill, and it always made an impression, but I don't like it. Instead, while at his base again I sucked hard enough that I couldn't open my muzzle if I tried, and began to drag upwards. The vacuum meant real resistance to him being pulled free, and he could feel every inch of himself gradually escaping me. Finally I hooked my lips behind the ridge of his glans and tugged playfully, licking over it, before doing the suction trick on the way down.

Thankfully I made it all the way back up without getting him off, but he was breathing hard and I tasted pre. Usually I hope for that because it makes a date much quicker, but in this case it would have colored the evening with an even more sour hue. Besides, while I wanted to show him some very good head, I had more I wanted to give him.

While teasing him I reached into my purse, pulled out and started opening the condom so that as soon as I lifted my head, I started rolling it down. He looked down at it then at me, but stayed quiet.

After making sure it was snug I gave him a little time to cool off. Leaning back, I peeled down my capris. I preferred to tease a little, undress slow, but there was just no room. It would've also been more discreet had I worn a skirt, but I wasn't expecting action.

"Could you scoot your chair back?"

Once he had I worked at maneuvering above him, tucking my knees into the sides of his seat, and I hooked my calves under his legs. A tight fit, but my ass wouldn't be honking the horn in the middle of the commotion. I sat back, leaving him pressed between our bellies, and caressed along his chest and stomach.

Jacob finally touched me, grazing my side like I was some soap bubble that might pop from too firm a nudge. I arched and smiled. "You're handsome," I told him. "If we were somewhere else, I'd have wanted to sit and cuddle." Which was true.

He cupped my breast and I pushed into it. "Really? I like to do that—cuddling."

"Yes." I drew the "s" sound into a breathy hiss as he began to toy with my nipple, encouraging him to keep touching me, to let go. "You're good at that. Have you been with a girl before?"

"Yeah." Jacob chuckled like the memory was a bad joke.

Deciding not to ask further, I started to rock, pressing our stomachs together and teasing his cock between our hot bodies, but he leaned up and started sucking on my nipple, making me jerk in surprise. I moaned for him, stroking one of his ears, and slid my body over him, hoping it wouldn't uproot the condom.

After rubbing the whole of my front across him, I rocked back and sat up, cupped him and pressed the condom-wrapped tip against my folds. Then I waited until I caught his eyes with mine. The skyline had grown dark blue so the lighter qualities of our fur and our eyes stood out the most. I gazed down into his, gave him a slow, sumptuous smile, and eased my weight down, sinking him into me.

He groaned, watching himself disappear inside. For his viewing pleasure I rolled my hips sideways like a pendulum on a clock as I went until I nestled on his lap. He felt good inside me, filling me up without the discomfort that a bigger species might bring. Flexing my muscles inside drew a startled breath out of him.

Being in no hurry, I leaned down and laid across his chest, wrapped my arms around his neck, and kissed him. This time the kiss lasted longer, his muzzle more enthusiastic against mine while his hands roved down my back and then squeezed my butt. I encouraged him, rocking side to side again, the motion stirring him inside me and making me shiver while my insides clenched in flutters.

Then I sat up, sliding back and grinding forward in a roll as I reached up and pressed my palms to the roof. Bracing, I started to churn my hips in a tight circle, stirring him around inside of me. I arched, pushing my breasts out. It tightened all those muscles along my front, too, making everything a display. Why yes I am a showboat; it comes with the territory.

Not that I had long to perform.

Beneath me Jacob snorted his chugging breath, his hooves shuffling against the floor mat. As I moved, his thighs and stomach tensed underneath me. He wasn't going over this second, but soon, and I knew I wouldn't be getting off. Long ago I'd accepted that orgasms were an uncommon bonus, like a compliment from your boss.

I started to bounce, and still bracing on the ceiling, pushed back down with my arms. My butt slapped against his thighs as the car started to really rock under the effort. Leaning back just a little, all my weight kept coming down on his pelvis and I knew the pressure would be intense for him even before I heard the sudden grunt.

A few more flexes of my thighs and he huffed a few heavy gasps through his teeth, his ears went back and I felt him twitch underneath me. Squeezing him on the inside, I slowed down but kept going, giving him something to watch and some nice friction as he wound down.

When his muscles unclenched and his face slackened to drowsy contentment, I stopped and lay on top of him. For several moments he hugged me, stroked the fur down my back, and kissed me. A lazy, comfortable play of muzzles and I melted into it.

Distant popping and clapping lifted my ears.

I peeked out of a window but didn't see anyone watching us. Light in the side-view mirror caught my eye, and I peered out the back window.

Jacob asked, "What is it?"

In the distance I saw the blossoming lights of fireworks.

"Nothing important," I said with a smile I rubbed into the line of his throat. But it felt like a sign of a job well done.

We parted and dressed, driving the rest of the way home. The chat was minimal. Jacob seemed relaxed and not self-conscious, but I could tell he was lost in thought or decompressing from everything. I didn't get the vibe he had illusions of a relationship between us; some clients got attached fast and hard and it was difficult every time. Others were ready to discard me along with the used condom. While not my type he was someone's, and I hoped he'd realize that one day.

In the quiet I mulled over what I did and what I was thinking of doing. I don't see any great nobility in what I do; I don't have that heart of gold, as the cliché says. But I want to try and meet the client's needs. He wanted to look good for his family, but underneath that I could see a hunger for acceptance and the intimate contact of someone else. He wanted to be wanted and liked, just like everyone else. That didn't come without something first though, and that I couldn't give him, only nudge him that way.

When we neared the hotel, I made my decision. "Jacob." His ears perked. "Doing this job, dealing with a lot of people, I've gotten good at reading them." Softening my voice and turning to face him, I asked, "You don't feel very good about yourself, do you?"

"What? No, no I feel fine," he said in the same tone he used when dodging the uncomfortable questions back at the barbeque.

"I think you have a low opinion of yourself. You shouldn't; you're sweet, and you make me feel comfortable." I reached out and laid my fingers on the back of his hand. "But I have the feeling you don't believe me. Some girls I know—they don't feel good about themselves at all, and no matter what they do, they still beat themselves up. They only see the bad. Until you're happy with yourself, nothing will truly make you happy."

He didn't respond, instead focusing on pulling into the parking lot beside my car. When he stopped, I nudged his muzzle so we could make eye contact. "I think you should talk to someone."

"Like a therapist?" He recoiled. "I'm not crazy."

"No, but they do more than that. They give you perspective. Fresh eyes on what's going on." I held back when I saw that expression that said he was thinking about it but leaning away. I couldn't ask him to do it for me, because I was going to disappear. But I wanted him to do it. When our eyes met, I leaned in and added, "It helped me when I needed it."

"Okay," he said, but I couldn't be sure he was convinced.

The discussion at least distracted him from one of those fumbling conversations at the end of the date. It gave me the window to end things casual and brisk. With a kiss to his cheek, I snagged my purse and slid out of the car. "Thanks for a good time."

"Good time?" He snorted. "Neither of us had fun back there."

"Oh, I didn't enjoy your family. But the time I spent with you?" I cranked up the wattage on my smile. "Have a good night, Jacob."

As I climbed in the car, he said, "I already did."

I watched him drive away and smiled to myself.

TEETH

The lioness bares her teeth in a smile at me and I shiver, knowing what's coming. When her strong hands take my shoulders and pin them to the mattress, I hold still except for the tremble of anticipation in my belly.

Leaning in close Carli runs her chin against my long muzzle, then parts her mouth just enough a line opens in her pearly whites. This she fits my jaw into before tilting her head to the side, to drag the points along my mouth. My nipples are so hard now, and I'm sure she can smell my arousal.

When her lips meet the base of my muzzle they delve down, and her maw opens this time, wide and full over my throat. I whine despite myself even before I feel the points along my delicate neck, before they press down with a mother's tenderness. The frantic jump of my pulse against her tongue must be so obvious, as clear as the damp shine of excitement on my thighs.

For who knows how long, her jaws run along my neck, because I could not keep track. *Hurry up, just give me something*, I think. As if she could hear me, she draws back and with a casual pinch she nips my shoulder. I moan.

To be her lips, her tongue, so that I spent every day nestled against her sleek, dangerous ivory.

Those points pluck at my upper chest, capturing a bit of fur and skin beneath to tug. My back arches and my tail, knowing wagging is too undignified of a wolf, brushes and stirs along the sheets. Trailing down my upper chest, Carli takes her time with each snag, holding me and wiggling, before pressing in until I whimper and curl my toes and a small part of me fearfully wonders, like I've done a hundred times before, if she'll break the skin.

Does Carli's dentist know just what the lioness is packing? The perfection she's hiding behind her lips?

This hot trail finds the peak of my breast. I glance down to watch as she traces the bare skin with each little tooth, only taking the nub fully into her mouth once she has. I get a glimpse of her golden eyes looking up at me from the shadow of dark curls, then she tries to take my whole breast into her mouth. It won't fit, but Carli always tries, and she draws back so slow, letting me feel every point.

Now I growl and struggle. Not to say I want her to stop, but to demand more right now.

In all her feline cruelty, Carli leans back and grins down at me, flashing me all her chompers. Any time I see those points, when she laughs or yawns or is burning mad, my tail hikes of its own accord and I want to pant.

Seeing them now I dampen the sheets, and know it's coming now. So I say, "Come on, eat me."

Her chuckle is smoke and honey. "Here I come."

The lioness wedges her thigh between my own, putting the power of her taut lower half into the grind against my heat. She pounces then, taking my throat to grip, to growl. If she had our strap-on Carli would take my scruff, but this is even better. I gasp and hold still, even as my insides vibrate like a plucked guitar.

Carli's whole body rolls, letting her thigh drag between mine like a violin's bow, even as her upper body rocks, giving subtle shakes to her muzzle. It's left me panting, and I feel it all building, building.

In that moment Carli's muzzle closes enough to stop my breath. Realizing I can't breathe, my stomach jumps and I fight. Even as I fight, I come, and muffled as I am I cannot wail my delight. I'm not finished before she lets me breathe, and I spend the last moments of the rush clinging and pushing against her, in echo of a fight and in approval.

She relaxes, lying on top of me to nose my neck as I catch my breath, her hands now carresing my shoulders at the sites of her biting.

I seize her arms and roll her over, my tail high and my mouth close to hers. We share a look, a grin, and then I lick her cheek in a long lap.

"Oh," Carli groans. "That tongue."

That tongue lolls in a pant before I put it to work, taking my turn.

WHEN THE PAINT DRIES

In between classes Luis glanced at his cell phone and his heart nearly leaped out of his mouth at the name beside the missed call.

Angel. She'd left a voice mail too.

Something must be wrong, something must've happened for her to call him. With a held breath he started the voicemail.

"Hey Luis, this is Angelita. I know it's been a while… would you like to have dinner this week? Catch up? Give me a call back."

His nose crinkled. She must want something. While they hadn't been hostile since the breakup, she hadn't been particularly warm, and he never knew his ex to "catch up" with anyone estranged for the sake of it.

Even knowing there were ulterior motives, Luis still hit the call-back button. Nothing. He tried once more before the next class bell rang. With a resigned sigh the cacomistle stuffed the phone in his pocket and faced the class.

The students tackled the assignment with a snail's enthusiasm, and he didn't blame them; his eyes kept shifting to the clock, urging it forwards. He did this during the last period of most days, but it being a Friday while he was waiting for that call made it all the worse. With a few minutes left, the high schoolers perched on the edges of their chairs. Luis passed through the row of stations, checking each drawing and making comments but in truth only paying lip service to the assignment.

"What 'bout me, Mr. Rojas?"

Might as well. With an inward sigh the ringtail stepped over to Tucker's desk. Luis always saved the mouse's drawings for last, and today's…whew.

A gallows set up in an empty square, a trapdoor open and a swinging noose. Rather than a medieval town though, the square had parked cars, neon signs, and other modern filler. Scattered around the ground were flyers with hashtags of some social outrage, discarded phones and protest signs.

"When I see this, I think—"

Tucker's ears went up and his features hardened, preparing to be called something he would likely revel in throwing back in Luis's face.

"—the perspective's off. The gallows here casts a big shadow, but nothing else does. And look at the windows and doors on this side of the square, they're smaller than those on the other side."

Tucker's scowl dialed back, but he still mumbled a sullen, "Yeah I see what you mean. But it's good?"

"Yes, it's good. Celebrate the good, but look for where it can be better."

Leaning in, Luis's tone went lower. "And if someone else sees this and freaks out, there's going to be a huge stink with the principle, and then I'll have to talk with the school counselor, some parents, even the media might get wind of it—it'll be a real pain in my ass. If you could ease up on the 'dark' stuff, for me, I'd appreciate it."

That earned him a smile, even if the kid's tone flipped back to sarcasm. "What, you want unicorns and rainbows and shi-uh, stuff?"

"Sure. As long as the unicorn has a flaming mane and

hooves, and the rainbow goes to a pot of gold held by a bikini model."

Now the mouse grinned, his piercings glittering. "Maybe."

He turned away and finished his rounds with a sigh. Yet another kid that left him walking on egg shells. Like the boy in second period who somehow worked a girl he crushed on into *every* project—it was creepy.

Back at his desk the ringtail waited out the long seconds with the rest of the class, and finally the bell released them to the wind. No answer on her phone. After the usual thirty minutes of paperwork minutia he packed up, hurried out the door and right into someone. All of his things spilled across the floor.

"Oh! I'm sorry." The raccoon joined him as he knelt to collect his things. "Hi, by the way," she said.

Luis stood back up and smiled at the other teacher. "Hi, Constance."

"So, um." She reached back, fumbling a neatly folded flyer from a back pocket. "I uh, I'm having a poetry reading downtown tomorrow, if you're free. And you want to come."

No wonder she wandered so far from her classroom. " I…don't think I will be, but I'll see what I can do," he said, taking the flyer. "And congrats on the reading. That's cool you don't just teach English, you take part, huh?" Inside he winced. That was so lame it left a bad taste in his mouth.

"Thanks, and maybe I'll see you there." At the sight of hope glittering behind her glasses, Luis's tail curled uneasily.

They smiled, she departed, and he lingered by the door. Her scent seemed heavier in the air than it should've been. Had she stood there, waiting to ambush him when he came out? The cacomistle dropped the flyer into the trashcan by the door. He coughed. All the way to the car he fretted about seeing her on Monday, her trying to politely milk out of him why he hadn't shown and telling him how she enjoyed it.

Constance was sweet, and cute, but…but…but nothing. There was honestly nothing wrong with her. Dating was a whole other world right now.

Fed up with Angel's lack of answer, he finally left a message. "Hey, looks like we're playing phone tag; I can't catch you. Call me back when you can please." All he could do now was turn the ringer on and wait.

Luis coughed as he pulled into his side of the duplex. Inside he changed clothes, grabbed a bottle of vitamin water and headed out back to his studio—little more than a big metal storage shed that scorched in the summer and held no heat in the winter. At least now the weather leveled off enough he didn't literally suffer for his art.

The first thing he spotted when he opened the big door was Angelita's unfinished painting. It stood as a constant accusation and an anchor pulling him down. It was a remake of the first painting he had made of Angelita, the one he'd been sketching when she noticed him in the off-campus pizza place she worked, the one he'd shown her the night they made love for the first time (which he suspected was the reason she had said yes in the first place), the first painting he'd sold. He'd been kicking himself ever since for letting it slip away.

No matter what he tried, Luis couldn't finish the painting—the memories and pain it drew up distracted him too much, and he always ended up dwelling on what drove them apart. He was too stubborn, she took everything personal, he wasn't serious enough, she needed all the control, she hated his pot smoking, he detested her friends, she thought she could change him and he didn't see a need to ever accommodate. Each barely tolerated the other's relatives. Near the end it seemed like an unending cycle of fighting and cold, unbearable silences. The irreconcilable issue of children finally broke them in half.

A set of coughs pulled him to the present, forcing him to realize he'd been standing in the doorway, staring at the painting again. Luis sighed and turned to his current project, setting the paints and brushes out. Even if the dream of a comic artist gig never materialized, he eventually fell into place working on book and magazine covers, even the occasional interior painting for roleplaying games. Photoshop had taken over the industry for the most part, but some still preferred it the old fashioned way. Over the next two hours his brush brought the dragon into being, the beast arching over the lake, fire fogging from its mouth onto the boat of warriors.

Back in the house for a dinner break, he was reaching for the stove when his cell phone wailed. The display read Angelita. Finally. He picked up and, after the initial pleasantries, Luis said, "You asked about dinner?"

"Yeah, I'm open any time this week and—"

A fit of coughs pushed past his lips.

Angie's sigh grated over him through the phone, as did the familiar annoyance in her voice. "When was the last time you did your inhaler?"

"Ah ah, you don't get to take that tone with me. You've got some other husband to hassle now," he chided, trying to sound playful.

She blew a raspberry. "Don't make me play the nurse card. When and where would you like to go out?"

Luis smiled, but his next thought soured it. "Is Doug coming along?"

"Just us. How about Pang Cho's tomorrow?"

One of his favorite restaurants? Alright, now something was up for sure. "Just to catch up, huh?"

A sigh whispered against his ear. "I want to talk about something, but a face-to-face thing, you know?" Her whiskers whooshed against the receiver; they only ever fanned out when her lips pursed in concern.

Luis's tail snapped. "It isn't cancer is it? Please tell me if it's some bad news. Waiting will just kill me."

"No! No, it's not bad. It's complicated and I want to see what you think about something." He could differentiate the lying tone from the blow-softening one. This was hesitation. What would she be cautious about, with him? "Please?" Now her tone had a small, almost needy tinge to it.

That did it. "Sure."

After they said goodbye he was left staring at the phone. Another coughing fit hit, and he finally went in search of his inhaler.

* * *

Luis sat on the bench in front of the laundromat next to Pang Cho's Lucky Best Restaurant, the rich aroma of sautéed food sending his begging to go in early. Since he'd last been here, a "for lease" sign had grown in the opposite storefront's window, as well as the street lamp developing a case of shattered lights. Without an excuse to go to Angelita's hospital, he had little reason to go downtown, and it looked like it had been that way for the rest of the city too.

The car that parked down the street didn't warrant his attention until she climbed out of it. Not brand new, but certainly not the ten year old model she had taken in the split. Luis stood and smoothed out his clothes as she came down the block. Not that he had to worry about appearances— poor Angel had the hollow eyes and sagged tail of a desiccating shift at the nurse's station, and primping in a bathroom after pulling off her duty clothes could only go so far. Still her smile lit him up when their eyes met, and the hasty combing and silly scrunchie didn't stop him from aching to run his fingers through her fur.

"Hey." She repositioned her purse onto her shoulder. "Did I leave you waiting long?"

"No, you're fine," he said and opened the door for her.

Even before the bell over the door finished chiming, a reedy voice called, "Mr, Mrs. Rojas!" The elderly dhole shuffled out from behind his desk beside the flowery wall divider and the bubbling fish tank. "Too long since I see you last, you both look good!" He still wore the same dinner jacket with the faded lapels, likely as old as the building itself.

"Thank you," Angel said. It pleased Luis to see her not even react to being called his wife, much less correct the old man.

Mr. Cho paused. "Did you hear about the child kidnapping at school?"

"No," Luis said deadpan, "what happened?"

"It was okay, he woke up." The dhole beamed his same proud smile.

Both cacomistles groaned, but the terrible humor was just another charm.

He led them to one of the twelve tiny tables in the back, the whole place lit only by tiny table lanterns.

Luis's ears flicked. "Did you change the music?" They were serenaded by sweet and lonesome vocals in another language, instead of the soft fluting notes that were as much a part of the place as those faded lapels.

"Tape broke. You no like? I can change—"

Luis quickly shook his head. "No, I like it, it's good." Despite Cho's skeptical eye, he accepted and backed away with their drink orders.

Sitting across from Angel messed with him, so used was he to having her on his right side. The table between them another reminder of the barrier. Picking here was a mistake – a hope for the nostalgic betraying him, because those pleasant old days were so distant, so different.

A silence between them stretched, disturbed only by Mr. Cho yelling to someone in the kitchen in his native tongue. The old man's wife appeared with their drinks. Her faded orange cheeks, dulled with age, shifted as she pursed her lips in thought. "Sesame chicken, and orange curry fish?"

Angel shook her head. "Just sautéed vegetables for me."

The ancient woman's mouth puckered like she just might disagree with deviating from the past.

"Yes, I'll take the sesame." That seemed to satisfy her.

When they were alone again, Luis asked about small things. New events, old friends, things that really didn't matter but they had to start somewhere. The rust and grit in the tracks of well-worn conversations shook loose before derailing.

"I'm—we're—thinking about having a baby." Those big, dark eyes bore into his.

A spike of alarm and discomfort lanced down Luis's tail. Hopefully he kept it off his face, as years of looking at poor art helped him hide that much. "Oh. That's…great. Are you going to look for a surrogate mother for Doug—"

"No," she shook her head, "I want to carry the baby."

He took a careful sip of diet soda. "Ah."

Discomfort saddled around her ears and she fiddled with her sleeve, a bad-news tell Angel had yet to break. "But I can't go to the sperm bank."

"Why not?"

She blew out a hiss. "Let me tell you about the director of the local place. He doesn't want to order out for any more donors, he doesn't want to go through the whole process because 'we have enough for you here'. I'll have to settle for one of the three ringtail samples they have there."

"What's wrong with them?"

She sniffed dismissively. "They're not impressive. I don't care for the donors' bios. And only three choices? I should have quality and I should have options, Luis. *Options.* This is a baby we're talking about, not the last bunch of bananas at the store.

"And going out of town is a nightmare. I'd have to go multiple times to make sure it 'took' and I don't have enough vacation days for it. Since there's so few cacomistles in this state it's hard to find a suitable donor, and I can't travel to where someone more suitable is for the same reason, so…." She met his eyes.

A thousand feelings rushed through Luis at once. Every fight they'd ever had about children, the loneliness of being apart from her, a bolt of joy at the possibility of having her back, of being used. Biting it all down, he choked on being calm. "You'd rather the donor be me."

It was her turn to bite down on something. "How do you feel about that?"

"I don't know Angie," he said, using the name she hated. "We haven't talked in what, three years, and you just drop by and ask me to squirt in a cup for you?"

"Vegetables and sesame," Mrs. Cho said as she set the plates down at the table.

Both ringtails recoiled, their ears hot. The old dhole acknowledged nothing, scooting the plates in front of them, one big bowl of white rice in the center, and somehow on tiny steps she darted away.

"So that's a no," Angel said once she regained herself, and stared daggers into her greens. Anger always hid her heartbreak.

"I didn't say that…" Thankful to have a distraction, Luis shoved spicy chicken into his mouth.

Her eyes came back up, an ember of hope sputtering inside. "It's complicated?"

"Yes," he managed after a hard swallow.

She stirred her fork around in the bowl, only gathering

food by accident. Those dark, pleading eyes dipped down. "If it helps, it wouldn't have to be in a cup."

A piece of chicken jumped down the wrong pipe. He waved her away from actually trying to stop him from choking, then spent several moments relearning how to breathe.

"I'm sorry, I think I misheard you," Luis said, his voice still hoarse. "Could you repeat that?"

Angel picked at her food. "Just that we could...try to make the baby the old fashioned way. If we used the clinic, there'd be the same issue. And before you ask, Doug knows about it. All of it."

With a shake of his head, he said, "Can I think about it?"

"Nothing's stopping you." Expected disappointment already poisoned her tone.

Luis had wanted to tell her how much he missed her, he had wanted to bring up good times, but now he could barely rub two thoughts together. The rest of the dinner went like that, a stiff weight wedged between every word and gesture.

* * *

"Thinking about it" meant trying every way in the world to distract himself the rest of the weekend. While he loathed to do it, he needed to talk to her husband. As soon as Monday's last bell rang Luis left school, driving to one of the few high rises in town.

Luis found Doug's office in the tiniest hole in the lowest rung of the fancy firm. He guessed Schuster, Shultz and Chavez didn't have a high opinion of small business law.

"Thanks for seeing me on short notice," Luis said as he sat down in the cramped office.

Doug didn't look up from his computer screen. "Quite alright. Hope you don't mind me working through this." The light of the monitor reflecting off his glasses gave him a hypnotized look. Or dullness, a drone-like blandness that went along with the rat's stiff suit, lifeless monotone, and an office barren of any personal touch. The room barely even smelled like him.

All the same vibe he picked up the one time he'd met Doug. Seeing Angel react with no starry-eyed contentment, nothing but warmed over familiarity told Luis all he needed to know: she was settling for the safety of a meek man in a secure job and now she wanted a family. Which also made no sense—if she wanted children, why didn't she marry another ringtail?

No sense in beating around the bush, or staying here any longer than necessary. "Angel wants me to be the father."

"It does make some sense. She said your family's health is good, you're creative, several important genetic markers."

Jesus, even his conversations were clinical. "Except for the asthma."

Doug shrugged.

"And it makes some kind of sense for her to not get pregnant in a clinic?"

Now the rat looked up from the monitor, and an actual personality peeked out. "Well, logistically the other route's a pain."

Luis tilted his head, his ears flicking forward. "But you don't *like* it?"

"No, that's quite fine. By letting her do this with you, I get uh, concessions of my own." While his tone remained colorless, Doug's muzzle drew at the corners into a grin and his eyes filled with the wicked amusement of men sharing lewd things.

Luis chuckled to hide his hiss. "I don't need to hear this." The words were honest even if the tone wasn't.

Another, weaker smile, before Doug turned back to his computer. "Sorry. But no, I don't have any concerns."

Luis could hear the message like it came from a bullhorn: I have no fear she'll leave me for you. He couldn't shake the underlying message they had went with him out of pure convenience. The thought left a sour taste in his mouth. The ringtail excused himself with a few pleasantries and disappeared.

* * *

Luis paced his living room as he listened to Angel's phone ring. Finally she picked up. "Hey."

"Can we talk, soon? About all of this?"

"Well, I want to but I don't think I can tonight, or tomorrow, but the next day, sure. Where?"

Luis paused a moment before saying, "My place?" Here we go.

After taking her turn to pause, Angel said, "I can do that."

Delaying for a few more days let him think. Or more accurately it allowed all his doubts and fears to chase his hopes in circles, leaving him distracted enough he needed to put art videos on in class rather than teach.

The ache for Angel was a constant thing, but would sleeping with her—creating a baby with her—make things even uglier? He hurt from her leaving now, could he handle her coming, making a child, and walking away again? Or if he got what he wanted, would they even last? Not to mention he didn't think Doug deserved losing his wife too, maybe the guy loved Angel as much as Luis did.

By the time her car pulled into his drive, Luis's insides had tangled up like old Christmas lights.

All of that temporarily disappeared as he watched her climb out of the car.

Angel may have agreed to talk, but one look told him she came for something else. She'd curled her dark hair until it bubbled down her shoulders, left practically bare from the tight red silk top. Tight, dark pants made her figure pop. He must have been down wind, because as she came up the walk his nose caught her. Under the day's travels he picked up a richer aroma that sent a tightness marching along his spine. That scent had only been present a few times in their marriage, and he'd treated it like a warning siren, but now he couldn't help being wound up and ready to spring from it.

He noticed she was watching him. Caught being very aware of her, Luis kept his ears low. "You look good."

"Thanks." Her eyes and smile turned coy. "For the last week I've…been taking some medications to get my body in gear, so I'm ready whatever ends up getting decided. It's only now settling in."

Was that why she wanted to delay? Wait for her cycle to rev up?

She slipped past him and inside. The way she held her tail didn't obscure her butt, an invitation to look that he took.

While she hovered in the middle of the room, Luis wandered to the couch. "So."

"So."

He coughed once, twice, and she rolled her eyes.

"Where do you see me in all of this?"

Angelita tilted her head. "Like what?"

"I mean, will I have any part in this kid's life? Would they even know who I was?"

Her nose crinkled and her eyes narrowed. "I thought you didn't want children in the first place?"

A tide of bitter emotions burbled up like bile. Not wanting kids hadn't just been the poison pill of their marriage, him not wanting them was *wrong*. Everyone was expected to pop out a litter to keep their species going, and he didn't want it. It was an embarrassment to his family. The pressure strangled them both, and he was the unreasonable bastard who wouldn't give in.

Luis choked it down. "I'm not exactly keen on changing diapers or losing nights of sleep, Angel, but I'd be happy going to Little League games or taking them trick or treating—I work with kids, I've gotten to like them." After a certain age, at least.

She opened her mouth and by the twist of her lips he knew it would be unflattering, so he interrupted with, "And you're going to need a babysitter. Often. You're going to need help."

Now he'd done it. The anger sparked behind her eyes when he suggested she'd need help. Angel needed no one. The way she told it, she came out of womb with a resume and clawed after everything she ever had, earning it through bloody trial. "I see. So you want all the nice things about parenting without doing any of the work."

He tried to keep calm. "So instead what you're saying is, 'please Luis do the most important thing you could ever do for me and our species, create another person, then get out of our life'? You can get that with the sperm donors, they've already signed their rights and concerns away."

She bit down on her next words and glared. It told him he had a point and she didn't want to admit it.

Why was he fighting? Was he trying to remind himself of what they were really like together, to take another dose of this poison so he didn't want to anymore? If that were true he knew it would never work, the stupid fool that he was.

"I didn't come here to start a fight." The tone of apology brought his eyes up to hers. Angel looked away while curling her tail around her legs in discomfort. "Those pre-natal drugs have put my hormones all out of whack and I'm…I nearly bit someone's head off at work. And it's good you're asking these questions, it's smart."

It was as close to an "I'm sorry" as he'd ever get out of her. "Even if I have a right to it, you still don't want me to."

"I don't know, Luis," she said with an exasperated puff raw with anxiety. "I didn't think you wanted to get involved. If I told you no, we were going to do the parenting by ourselves, would you still help me?"

It was his turn to sigh, and he flopped onto the couch. "I don't know either. Maybe? But I do want to get this stuff cleared up. I'm not saying split custody or anything, the baby should know who I am. It's not just the 'nice things', I'll do the work too." He looked away. "I'm afraid that when I'm old this'll be one more regret, that I let the kid slip away." Like her.

Angel rubbed her cheeks before sliding her fingers up into her hair. "Okay, we will settle this, but I think it's fair we all sit down and hash it out, Doug too. But…can we talk about it later?" An apologetic smile creased her muzzle, tinged with something else.

"And talk about something else?" he ventured, although his quicker pulse told him that wasn't the idea.

Angel leaned against the stair railing. "We could." A tiredness, or maybe just distraction, had entered her voice. "Or we could go upstairs. I'm a little…heh." She waved a hand and glanced away. "I think the meds made my heat worse than usual, uh, it's hard to focus, here."

"We could do that."

* * *

The warmth he found came only in the heat of her body, her touches and movements only enough of an echo to encourage him finishing. Only enough.

They stared at the ceiling as their barely-strained breathing wound down.

Angel asked, "Can I use your shower?"

"Yeah, sure."

She paused in the door. Once, the sight of her nude silhouette gazing back over her shoulder, with a slice of half-light highlighting the rumpled fur of her tail, would have been the inspiration for a sketch or a quick painting. He would have asked her to hold still so he could put it to memory. Instead he closed his eyes.

"Do you still use that awful off-brand shampoo?"

When the only answer she received was coughing, Angelita disappeared into the hall, leaving him lost.

* * *

After school Luis drove all the way down to Pang Cho's. He pushed rice around his plate.

A cold lump had formed in his throat since last night, one that warbled and nudged a hint of wetness to his eyes every time he thought about Angelita.

Mrs. Cho set the tray with the fortune cookie and the check down at his table and claimed his spent plate without a word. She stepped back and right into Mr. Cho, who had just seated someone.

They turned and he caught two sour faces narrow in minute glares. They said nothing, parting in equal withered distaste. They must hate one another, but stuck there all those years together.

Like him and Angel would have.

Luis could see it, the two of them drying up like bitter prunes, brined in domestic toxicity. Whatever it was that didn't make them work, Angel knew it and didn't look back. He should've seen it, couldn't see it.

If he couldn't have Angel, then should he bother with the baby? Would it be just as brittle if he kept coming around, a frosty exchange in parking lots and weekends?

It had been him who didn't want them. He'd denied her,

denied their species' duty, because he was afraid. Afraid of doing the wrong thing, afraid of losing them, afraid of not being able to support them on his shitty income. It had been so easy to tell himself they would make terrible parents considering how they made a terrible couple.

But Angel and Doug may not be.

It may have been fair for him saying no in their marriage, but it wasn't fair to say no now, when he didn't have to make any more sacrifices. Angel could push him out of their lives, but now he knew this time he couldn't simply walk away.

* * *

A mare he didn't know opened Angelita's door, the sounds of laughter escaping behind her. "Hi," Luis said. "I'm just dropping off a gift."

"Oh! Come on in, you're just in time. Angelita, there's a man here with a package for you!"

"Is it a stripper?" someone tittered from inside, followed by a chorus of giggles.

Luis hefted his present and brought it into a room covered in so much pink he thought a cotton candy machine must've exploded. Little clothes spread out all over the floor, along with a stroller and a high chair plastered in yellow ducks. He said hello to Angelita's sister and mother clustered among the other women, but his eyes never strayed far from Angel and her swollen belly.

"I wasn't expecting you," she said, her ears forward with curiosity. She glanced down to his hands.

Luis turned the painting around. The other women crooned in approval while Angel's eyes widened and she tried to sit up straighter. "Is that—"

"Not the original. Took me a while to repaint, but I

managed. Thought you should have this."

"But I…I remember how much you wanted the first one back." A hint of a glisten peeked at the corners of her eyes, but went no further. The brightness of her face though wasn't held back. "Are you sure you don't want to keep it?"

Luis glanced down to admire Angelita's portrait upside down. When his eyes came up, they met hers and he smiled. It brought to mind his date with Constance later that night. "I'm sure."

RICKETY V

When Beth had texted "There's something I need to talk to you about," Conner had been a little worried that something was up. When she'd then sent "There's someone I want you to meet," he expected maybe that meant her parents. That was odd, since they'd barely went out together, but no big deal.

So while he didn't have many expectations, he also didn't know what to make of the border collie in Beth's living room.

This was the first time he'd been to Beth's townhouse. Like her, it was slender and cute, right down to the smiling ladybug flowerpots dotting her little porch.

"Conner," Beth said at the door, the mink's usual warmth muted.

His tail wagged. "I like the flowerpots."

"Oh, thank you." A brightness came back to her eyes. "That was an art project, and some of the kids gave me theirs instead of taking them home."

He grinned. "I guess that's why one of them is sticking out a tongue?"

"And that would be Jeffrey Rudder's." Her words came out distracted as the mink glanced back into the cozy living room.

That's when he stepped inside and noticed the other dog.

The border collie stood with her arms crossed, tail still and stiff behind her. Her ears tilted at angles, a sign she was making an effort to keep them from folding back.

Beth lingered by the other dog. "This is Mis- this is Janine."

The cheerful smile he had brought sunk to a merely friendly one, but it didn't stop his tail from bouncing in a wag. "Hi. I'm Conner." Were his ears not floppy they would have perked. Instead his ears swayed as their bases lifted. He held out an arm.

"Hello," she said with a fake smile and extended her arm politely.

Dipping his nose to her wrist and sniffing, he picked up the scents of books and tea. She didn't smell him in return, crossing her arms when he was done.

"Was it windy when you came in? When I walked here my ears almost turned inside out."

Beth said, "I haven't been outside."

Janine's head tilted. "I hadn't noticed. Now that you mention it, I can hear it." The wind brushed against the walls and under the eaves.

They stood waiting for a break in the ice that never came. Beth finally said, "How about we sit?" Her voice held the forced cheer of trying to get listless kids excited. "Can I get you anything to drink? Water, soda?"

Declining, Conner slouched to one end of the couch. Janine perched rigidly on a chair at the couch's other end. Beth knelt at the collie's feet, then glanced up at Janine's face before taking the spot on the couch next to Janine. That was odd. Only later did it all seem like the mink sat between them to play referee.

He smoothed a palm over the couch's arm repeatedly, and behind him, through the tail-slot, he flopped his tail. The couch was the loudest color in the room, a sunny yellow that matched his golden fur.

Did they notice he wasn't sitting still? No, he needed to stop thinking like that; if he thought they thought he couldn't relax, then there was no way he could settle down.

Janine cleared her throat and crossed her legs. "Conner,

how did you two meet?"

"Well we'd already seen each other a lot. I'm a lifeguard at the gym." He shot a smile to the mink. "But I coach soccer too and she picked her nephew up from practice one day, and that's when we got to talking."

"Oh. That's nice," Janine said.

Conner winced and fidgeted. Everything Janine said had the tone of a parent responding to a kid with no interest at all. He could see it from a disapproving mother but this didn't make sense. He looked towards Beth but she wasn't meeting his eyes.

The border collie cocked her head. "Hold on. Her nephew, a mink, is good at soccer?" She sounded at least mildly curious.

Thinking about his team brought back a grin. "You'd think so, right? They're not really built for running and kicking, but Marcus's got the flexibility and reflexes to make a pretty decent goalie. And he's a good kid when he's paying attention."

Beth chimed in, "Marcus's pretty enthusiastic about playing."

The expression Janine gave Beth was friendly and pleased, but when she turned back to him it froze over. "Well that's good."

Either she was just an unpleasant individual, or something was up.

"Is everything okay?" He leaned forward, elbows on his knees. "You seem um, tense." That was the nicest way for him to phrase it. Conner wanted to ask if he had done something wrong, but maybe this wasn't his fault.

Beth and Janine shared a glance before the mink said, "We needed to tell you this together. She's my mistress."

Conner's forehead wrinkled. "But you're not even married."

Janine snorted.

Beth fidgeted with her tail. "In a...well, what we do is... she—"

"It's a sex thing." It came out of the collie like a challenge or a taunt, complete with a stare and raised chin, missing all but flattened ears and bared teeth. The furniture obscured their tails but he would have bet that hers was up.

Beth winced and shifted in place.

"Oh. Huh." He sat back, rolling that around in his mouth. "You didn't say you were seeing anyone. You're having sex but are you dating?"

"No." Janine's ears dropped like a brick.

Conner rubbed at his neck. "Then can *we* still date?"

"So you're okay with that?" The mink turned to face him more fully.

A shrug. "It's not a problem for me. If you like girls, I can't really be a girl for you."

"Wait." Beth cocked her head, for a moment showing him the stern teacher inside. "Are *you* having sex with anyone?"

His floppy ears flattened even more than regular. "Well not right now." A pause. "I mean not *right now* right now, y'know, but not lately either."

Like a light went on inside of her, Beth wheeled to Janine and beamed. "I told you this would work out. He's really nice and accommodating."

The border collie looked like she had bit into a lemon. All the wind went out of her and she sagged back into her chair. Her ears were up though, and she looked back at Beth.

Conner leaned forward. "This...mistress sex thing, is it the usual girl-on-girl stuff?" He almost said he'd seen enough videos to know what that was, but thought better of it.

Beth's whiskers splayed. "Not exactly, um." She looked to Janine.

The collie mumbled, "It's tying each other up, things like

that."

"Okay." He straightened up and perked his ears. "Well can you show me how to do that?"

"What?" they said together.

"If that's something Beth likes, then I want to at least given it a try, so that maybe I can do it too."

Janine's ears went half-mast as she stared at him. "Do you know anything about it, even whether the idea excites you?"

Conner shrugged. "If someone says 'here, taste this,' you take a bite. If you ask them what's in it, then you might never try something you like." A grin caught his muzzle. "Maybe I'll like it. So can you show me?"

Janine said, "No."

At the same moment, Beth said, "Sure."

The two women looked at each other, the collie's ears flattening back enough to disappear into her hair. "Well," Beth said, "she doesn't have to be there. You and I can do that together, um, privately."

"Now hold on. If this is something you two want, I should probably be there." Janine bit every word. "For no other reason than safety."

Beth started to slide off the couch, then paused, extending an arm out to the collie. When Janine nodded, as if giving permission, the mink slid off the couch and tucked herself against Janine. "Are you sure?" She bumped her nose against one of those down ears.

"I'm sure." Conner saw Janine smile for the first time. It was mixed in with heavier things, but it was there at Beth's touch. She sighed through her nose, and when the mink nipped her ear, he heard the collie's tail thump the chair's back.

Janine left soon after, and the moment she was out the door, Beth dropped onto the couch.

Conner reached over and rubbed one of her little

cookie-shaped ears. "I don't think she likes me very much."

She tilted into his touch. "I don't think it's you...mostly you, anyways. But no, this isn't a love triangle so much as a 'V'. A flimsy one." Turning to nose at his wrist, she bit him.

Conner jerked his hand back.

"Oh no, sorry." The mink sat up, her ears flushed. "I was being affectionate, it's a mustelid thing."

He rubbed at the spot, but smiled. "I was just surprised by how needle-y your teeth are. I'm sure I'll get used to it."

Beth slid alongside him and leaned against the dog. He naturally wrapped an arm around her, and Beth sighed, tucking her muzzle into his shoulder. Without looking at him she asked, "Sorry to dump all of that baggage on top of you suddenly. I wanted to tell you, but she wanted to meet you and get it all sorted out in person, and disagreeing with her is not easy for me."

"That was an ambush, yeah. At least you told me."

She scratched behind one of his ears, getting him to thump his tail. "I was worried it would scare you off, or give a bad early impression."

"Not yet." Squeezing her, Conner said, "I would like to hang out more, go out on an actual *date* date." The look on her face made him add, "Not tonight though. You look wrung out."

"Emotional day." Beth smiled weakly. "I'm so fried that I'm being blunt on top of everything else. But I would love that," she said with warmth. "How about dinner tomorrow?"

He nosed her forehead. "Sure. I probably should go. Let you recuperate."

As he shifted to get off the couch, she clung to his arm. "Wait. This is going to sound stupid but...I'm well, Miss and I are sharing so much right up front. It makes me feel vulnerable and, can you do me a favor and tell me something embarrassing about you?" She peeked through her bangs at him. "Nothing deep and dark."

It didn't take him long to find something. "I believed in Santa Claws until I was thirteen."

Beth blinked and made the face he knew she would. "That's…pretty old."

He sighed. "I know. But my parents were kinda poor, they were always talking and fighting about money, so I figured there was no way they could buy all the stuff me and my brothers got. Nobody was giving it to us, and Santa seemed the only option." His ears lifted. "I didn't realize that my parents saved all year. My mom really wanted us to believe in the magic of childhood. So I did what I could to help make the next couple of Christmases magical too."

Beth's eyes sparkled. Leaning in, she brushed her nose against his. "I think that'll do."

* * *

Cecil's Fish Fry smelled of fish and tartar sauce, but mainly of delicious grease. A chalkboard declared "Catch of the Day Special," but since they were hours from the ocean, Conner doubted there were any real "catches." It was louder than he'd expected, a competition between the jukebox and the chatter, interrupted by a bear yelling out order numbers. Another bear had taken their order. Must've been a family place.

Conner dropped into the booth with his drink and checked their number again.

Beth set down napkins, cups of tartar and cocktail sauce, ketchup and a dozen other options. It was a surprise she let him fetch his own drink. "You didn't have to do that."

"I know, but I like to." She slid into the booth beside him, her words intimate in the noise. "So, what're you thinking?"

His ears drooped. That question never got any good reactions, because he was usually not thinking of anything particularly deep. "Um. There's a lot fewer otters here than I expected." He could see only one among all the cats, raccoons, and an older mink couple.

"Fish is more popular than you'd think," Beth said with a smile. She glanced around, then tucked herself in closer. "But I meant…have you thought over what we talked about yesterday?"

"Some. I tried looking stuff up last night and wound up on a site about rubber suits? That's not your thing is it?"

She laughed. "No, no. And questions are good. But I can't answer all of them. Miss ordered me to just tell you about the basics, because she wants to handle things. And this place is loud enough I don't think anyone would overhear us too much."

"That's a place to start. If this is a sex thing, then why are you taking orders outside the bedroom?"

"It's not just sex, it's…." She splayed her whiskers, squirming. "I don't want to be pampered, but I like this idea of being someone's little princess, their doll. Being held, or made to look pretty just for them. It means I have their total attention. When I'm following orders, it's like being held by someone bigger than me, but they can do it from across town. It makes me feel special."

Conner bobbed his head. "That makes sense. Does this mean I should get you a little tiara?"

The face she made got a laugh out of him once he was sure she didn't mind the teasing. Beth wasn't the sort to playfully hit him or laugh at something so intimate about herself, but her eyes shone with the humor of it.

Conner said, "But I don't know anything about this, so what do you see in me?"

The mink glanced away and sighed.

"Seventy four!"

Conner perked at the number, but Beth shot out of the

booth.

The basket of deep-fried fish and chips dropped in front of him, the grease and sea salt smell rich and intoxicating, mingling with the aroma of shrimp coming from her side.

Beth slid in across from him this time, perhaps to better eat, or was the intimate talk over? Wanting to see if she'd bring it up, he waited, watching her in between cutting into his fish.

Nothing. The smell drove him to take a fork-full, and he almost had it in his mouth before the mink said, "Hey wait. You're not going to have it with vinegar?"

"Vinegar?"

"Haven't tried that on fish before?"

His nose wrinkled. "I thought the only thing vinegar went on was like, salad."

"Here." Plucking up one of the condiments collected earlier, she broke the seal with a claw and squirted the strong-smelling contents onto a napkin. "Now, dab that on this."

He did as instructed, and the taste zinged along with the sea salt. Odd, unexpected, and it made his tongue wiggle at the thought of pickles on fish, but it was still good. The rest of the malted vinegar went on his meal.

"So, what I asked earlier—"

"You want these?" she asked, gesturing to the balls of fried cornbread.

"I'm good," he said, waving one of his own, before chomping it. "You don't like talking about you much."

Beth's whiskers fanned around her mouthful of shrimp. Focusing very hard on her dinner she said, "I don't know what people will think about me. In this case it's kind've bad."

"Some people have told me I don't think a whole lot, so I think you'll be safe."

She shot him a smile, but turned it back on her shrimp. He let her chew and think. "You're kind of the first male I've been interested in."

That raised his ears. "No one else's been attractive?"

"That's where the bad thing comes in. Attracted to, yes, but guys intimidate me." She squirmed. "It's sexist but if a male you barely know is being nice to you, he's usually sniffing around for sex. By the time I was friends with the ones who were happy being friends, I was with someone or we don't mesh well, or a dozen other things. And I'm not exactly the most outgoing girl, out there looking, you know. You though, you were into me but I thought you wanted to be friends. Even before you said anything I was already impressed with you."

Conner cocked his head. "How?"

"The day I came to pick up Marcus, I watched you with the kids. I could tell they adore you. Marcus says you're not like an adult but a big ten year old. Even when you're in charge, he feels listened to and respected."

That set his tail wagging, and his chest hurt from the pride bubbling up. "They're people, just smaller. Their feelings and problems are real to them. Parents are either too overprotective or they dismiss them for being young. I try to be fair."

Beth's eyes lit up. "And that's why I wanted to go out with you. Anyone that nice to kids must be pretty good."

He reached across and stroked her arm.

She cleared her throat. "The sexual attraction didn't hurt either. I had a feeling you could be soft and not-so-soft. I want to be treated very gently, and romantically. Until I don't want to be." Her smile was full of shy suggestion.

Under the table, he brushed his foot alongside hers. "Oh. Well, you're pretty good at sensing this stuff then, 'cause I think I can do that." They shared an intimate grin.

He licked his nose. "Wait. If you've never been with a guy, how do you know you like anything rough?"

"Because the right ladies aren't gentle if you ask them nicely."

The thoughts that stirred left his tail wagging. "Oh."

"Great." She sighed with relief. "Now maybe we can get away from sharing secrets for five minute."

* * *

Conner paced from the far wall of Beth's living room to the end of her kitchen. After a brief talk about BDSM that left him with more questions, Beth intentionally avoided answering and disappeared upstairs to get ready, leaving Conner to wait alone.

At her knock, Conner opened the door and let the border collie in. She wore a leather vest, tight jeans, and boots. It was hard not to look at her very presented cleavage, but Janine's serious expression and the way she stood, tail and ears up, shoulders forward, helped a hell of a lot. "Hi. Beth's still getting ready—"

"Good. I need to have a word with you first. Sit." He did so. "What did Beth tell you?"

He shrugged. "Just what a safeword was and the difference between a dom and a sub. General stuff, I guess. She wouldn't tell me much of what she's into, because you told her not to." That last point left a bit of annoyance in his tone.

"That's right, because I'm running the show, and I want to do it right the first time. Now first I want you to know I'm uncomfortable." The border collie seemed taller, and despite her even tone Janine's eyes held back more than frustration. "I don't like this, but I'm going to do it anyways because that's what being an adult is about. Secondly, tonight I'm going to come off as a bitch. That's not because of anything going on here, between us. It's just part of the game. Don't be defensive, don't take it personally, just try to roll with it. If you're unhappy, or uncomfortable, safeword. If you want to just slow things down, say yellow. Got it?" The lecture came out smooth and confident, like she'd rehearsed it.

He bobbed his head. It was simple enough, and he gave a smile. "Thanks for being up front and clear. I appreciate it."

"Yes, well…." She raised her voice. "Beth?"

The mink slinked down the stairs, a slow sway rippling through her body like a snake. On some other species it would've come off as an exaggeration, slutty as hell, but she glided with ease. Conner had seen few people move like that outside of movies, and he'd never expected it from Beth.

She wore matching lingerie—bikini panties, stockings, and a camisole all in maroon. The material was see-through, and went great with her dark fur. He couldn't tell whether the material over her nipples and between her thighs wasn't clear, or if her fur's color kept her decent. The outfit left her stomach and thighs bare in all that maroon, and his fingers flexed with a need to touch those uncovered spots, to peel her clothes off, to have all of her right then.

One look at the border collie's face told Conner they at least had that need in common.

"Miss, can I get you something to drink?"

"No, that's fine." Janine clapped her hands once. "Alright, first thing's first. We need to negotiate. Girl, sit."

Conner already sat on the couch's end where he had a few days before, and Beth moved to the other end, but Janine barked, "Girl, on the floor."

Beth ducked her head and knelt.

"Good." Janine took the chair.

Conner cocked his head. "Why does she need to kneel on the floor?"

"It's stage dressing, reminds everyone she's not on the same level as you and I."

His ears did their best not to go back. Were all these mind

games what he'd gotten himself into, all for sex? "This seems really complicated."

Janine smirked. "You said you coach soccer? That's really complicated for just kicking a ball around."

He ducked his muzzle. Maybe she had a point, but damn. "Okay."

The collie wrinkled her muzzle thoughtfully, rubbed her eyes, and said, "But you do have a point, I'm falling into old habits. Beth, we don't need to use our degree of protocol for this. That's up to him. So stay there but you don't need to kneel. And face him, this is between you two."

Turning, the mink curled her legs beneath her and propped on a hand. If it wasn't so casual looking he'd have thought she was striking a pose. How was she acting so different, so naturally sexy? The shyness was there, but it had taken a back seat.

She shot him an encouraging smile. At least she looked interested in going forward. With her like this, he was very interested.

"Conner, you ask her what kind of kinks she's interested in."

He shifted on his seat. "What kind've sexual stuff are you into?"

"Well, I do kind of like bondage—that's tying people up. Does the idea of tying me up sound hot?"

Conner licked his nose in nervousness. "I like tying with my knot."

Janine snorted. Beth hid an annoyed look from the collie by smiling at him. "Not quite the same thing. I can also be a bit of a pain slut."

His expression must've said something because Janine added, "What she means is you can bite her or spank her. If you like that, we'll teach you how to do more."

The idea of pain feeling good seemed backwards until

he remembered how she showed affection with her teeth, and that it wasn't really so bad. Maybe it was like the ache after a workout—it felt good because of the accomplishment, because your body was worn out, not injured. Hadn't he put batteries on his tongue as a kid? He could do that.

"Anything else?" he asked.

"I'd like it if you were rough." She made eye contact, even lifted her muzzle. "Push me, hold me down." The idea of it, and her saying it, finally had him getting hard.

Janine sat up straight. "Is that a new interest?"

Beth's eyes dropped to the floor. "No, Miss."

"Since when, then? I don't remember this."

The mink started to close off, to curl in on herself. "I thought this was about helping Conner." A single note of soft scolding entered her voice. Probably her only way of complaining about the collie's behavior. "Do we need to talk about this—"

"Yes, Girl." Even as the volume dropped, Janine's tone turned as sharp as cat's claws.

Beth trembled. Her voice came away nervous and guilty. "I told you during our first negotiation, but you weren't interested in that."

The collie looked like she'd been slapped. Before she could say anything though, Conner stood up and barked at Janine, "Hey. Is this what this is all about? Because she doesn't look like she's having any fun."

Janine's mouth opened and closed several times, her eyes flicking between them, before she took a deep breath and made the effort to relax. "This isn't fun every moment. Sex isn't always fun or perfect every time, either."

"No, but…but…." He looked to Beth for help, and when none came, he sat down. "It seems like you're making up reasons to be upset."

The collie was back to playing teacher. "Like any game,

sometimes you're out, you don't perform well, you're penalized. Everything that goes on is what we agreed on because we like it. Sometimes though, we make mistakes, like I just did. I wasn't fair." She leaned in and stroked Beth's hair. "I'm sorry."

Beth nuzzled into her touch, but her eyes were on Conner. "Do you still want to keep going? This doesn't seem to be working for you."

He dug fingers through his neckfur. "Some of what you're talking about is hot, but I don't know what I'm supposed to do here. All I do know is that I don't want to yell at you, or make you sit in a certain place, or whatever else goes in the opposite direction of making you moan."

Janine said, "Let's all take a moment to breathe and think." She stood and paced the room.

Closing his eyes, he leaned his head back and relaxed. He could bail out now. No one would blame him. Still, he was kind of excited, and he had a sense that underneath all the "stage dressing" there was something he would like. Failing to do this would probably ruin any relationship chances. If he was honest, Conner really wanted to have sex with Beth, and going home unsatisfied would be very disappointing on top of everything else.

A clap brought his ears up. Janine said, "How about we try one more time. Conner, I want to get you in the right mindset. Beth, will you let him do anything he wants to you?"

"Yes. Well, if I don't, I'll safeword or you'll stop him."

"Right," Janine turned back to him. "I want you to assume you can do anything you want to her, and she'll like it. If you want to touch her, then do it. If you want her to do something, tell her and she will. She can say no, but you're so vanilla I highly doubt you'll cross a line."

Conner cocked his head. "Did you just call me ice cream?"

"Focus. Look at her and tell her to do something that will

turn you on."

Gazing down at the mink on the floor, he blurted the first thing that came to mind. "I want you to come up here with me."

Beth smiled with flirtation and rose, putting an extra roll in her hips before she sat sideways in his lap. That hadn't been what he meant, but he definitely didn't mind, and reflexively he put an arm around her.

"Good." Janine actually sounded pleased. "Now do something to her that you want to do."

After a moment's hesitation he cupped the mink's breast. She pressed into it, her eyes half-lidding.

It was then she became aware of his erection, glancing down at their laps first before experimentally rubbing her thigh against him.

Beth licked her lips. "It helps me get into the right mood if there's something I can call you. I call her Miss because Mistress is so clunky. Is there something you'd like?"

"Does 'Sir' work?" He always took a bit of weird pleasure when adults called him that.

"Yes, sir." Pushing her breast into his palm, she started to rock against his bulge. For being inexperienced with guys, she was excellent. "Will you tell me what excites you, sir? What do you look for in porn?"

The one good thing about floppy ears was no one saw when his went hot. Was this the same shy girl who squirmed when he asked her questions? "I like clothes. Sexy outfits, like what you're wearing now, and…you said you like being someone's doll, so then maybe I'll dress you up so I can undress you."

The grin he got was pure heat. Beneath his fingers her nipple was like steel. "I love dress up. Is there anything else I can do for you?"

"Will you…." He clearing his throat and started over.

"Open my pants." The restrictive khaki was killing him at this point.

Straddling his thigh, she glanced down at his lap and hesitated. Was she starting to get uncomfortable? The slow touch of her fingers tracing his bulge wasn't uneasy, just inexperienced and exploring. Whether she meant to or not, the time she took in unbuttoning and peeling his zipper was cruel.

Finally the red-pink shaft escaped into the air. For a moment Beth stared at it, then daintily stroked it.

He held back a growl. Did she need to be so slow and soft? Conner pinched her nipple and tugged it, earning a startled sucking breath. "I like talking. Especially hearing you say dirty things."

She glanced up, voice turning careful. "Talking is okay, but I don't like being humiliated. No name calling like 'slut.'"

Conner's ears went back. "No, no. I mean like um." With his free hand he took the back of her head and nudged down, forcing her to look at his cock. "I want to hear where you want me to put this."

Beth stared at his erection, then her eyes lifted to meet his through her bangs. "I need this in m-my pussy." That last word fumbled past her lips like she wasn't used to swearing, but he couldn't miss the excitement. "I'd like to put it in my mouth sometime, and I've had toys under my tail before so that could happen, but tonight, will you please…fuck my pussy, sir?"

Behind Beth came a soft strangled noise.

Janine had completely disappeared from his world, and she came back into it not looking good. Not even aware they'd noticed her, she stared at a wall with ears back and shoulders stiff enough to hold up furniture.

Beth had noticed too, tilting her head to discretely look at Janine. Concern slipped under her features and she met his eyes.

He coughed. "Uh, Beth, if we're going to really do this, I'll need a glass of ice water for later. Canine thing"

The mink slipped off his lap and walked without her previous slink. As she passed Janine she brushed fingers along one of the dog's ears.

It startled Janine, but she smiled after Beth. Her attention turned back to him, noticed his package, and quickly stared at a space a foot from his face. Clearing her throat, she said, "You seem to be doing better." Was that a shake in her voice?

"I guess, yeah." That had went well, right? It was all about being in charge. He could do that, had to be when coaching. Since he worked with kids though, acting like a coach was the wrong way to think about it.

He should say something. With Beth out of the room, it might be easier. "You don't look too great though. Would you like us to stop or slow down or—"

"I. Am. Fine." Janine bit every word.

They sat in a thick and thorny silence. After a minute, Beth had yet to come back, and every moment was like being at the dentist. What could he say to make Janine feel better, to make this at all easier?

Finally the mink came into view carrying two glasses. Conner caught the smell of something alcoholic and fruity before Beth stopped by the border collie and nudged her with the small glass. "Thank you," Janine said and immediately took a pull.

Beth nosed at the collie's ear before pulling away. She handed him the cool glass. It was his turn to take a heavy swallow, the cool water helping.

Leaving most of it for later, he stashed it on an end-table. Conner leaned back to offer his lap again but she didn't take it. Instead she met his eyes and touched a breast, trailing her fingers to her exposed stomach and along one hip, brushing her panties' front before caressing a thigh. "What do you want?"

"You." Cupping her hips, Conner leaned in and licked her thigh where she'd stopped the trail, and he followed it with his mouth, nuzzling between her legs before kissing higher. A soft chirr vibrated her chest by the time he nosed between her breasts. Back to her underwear, he snagged the waistband and inched them down her legs, touching her the whole way until they'd reached her shins. He palmed her calves and stroked upwards as he kissed his way between her thighs.

Even after the intermission her dark folds were damp. The smell was electric and as spicy as her taste. The second lick drew a gasp and it only made him hungry to hear more, scooping up her pert rump to pull her closer. He didn't ease up until she writhed, clutching his ears to stay steady.

Sitting back, Conner snatched her hips and turned her around before yanking the mink into his lap. Beth chirped in surprise but merely nodded when he said, "Roll your hips." The silk of her fur rubbing against his renewed erection curled his toes. An impulse had the dog grab her by the hair and pull, exposing her throat. The groan she let out encouraged him on and he buried his mouth in her throat. Somewhere in there his shaft became tucked snugly between her cheeks, and they ground together, the velvety sensation fluttering across his hot skin. His hand slid around her, under her, and started the tease up again.

The mink bent in his grip and he caught a glimpse of Janine with her hackles up, clutching the glass like the safety rail of a rollercoaster.

"Sir, sir," Beth huffed breathlessly, "do I have permission to come?"

His muzzle lifted. "Huh?"

"I-I uh, when it's time, am I allowed to orgasm?" Her thighs squeezed his hand. "I'm not there yet but maybe soon."

"Um, yeah. Yes. I mean err, you have permission." Those

last few words attempted authority, but the stumble had him wincing all the same.

While keeping her butt firmly planted in his lap, Beth pivoted around and kissed him. Where most people could only turn their shoulder back and look behind them, she twisted at the waist until most of her chest was against his, then threw an arm around his neck and met his mouth.

If he hadn't seen her nephew do tricks like that at practice, or weasels in action movies, it would have freaked him out. Instead he quickly got over the surprise and sank into the kiss. They both were experienced enough with different muzzle shapes to have little difficulty kissing.

Their mouthes broke when he tapped her clit and she jerked free to gasp. Conner shoved his free hand under her hair and seized her scruff. Beth arched her back and hissed blissfully, clenching her butt around his dick.

Rough, she'd said. Push her around.

Conner came half off the couch as he twisted, shoving Beth face-down into the couch. Yanking her nape again had her on her knees, and he herded her to the couch's arm, forcing her half across it. Beth instinctively spread her legs and presented with her tail hiked to the side.

He could do this. This was great. Too many times he'd wanted to just throw a girl over the nearest surface and take her like something feral, but he'd held back because it would scare her or they were in a store or it was wrong to do that to strangers. Nothing held him back now, and it felt as if something deep inside puffed out its chest and howled like a primitive wolf.

Several inches were buried in her before the tightness and a sharp squeak reminded him this was Beth's first time with a guy. Conner paused in concern, but she urged him on with a backwards nudge. Little resistance met his more careful next push. He gave one full stroke into her before breathing, "That okay? Good?"

"Yes," she growled shakily. "More… fuck me sir, please, I need this."

By the time his hips nestled fur to fur with her ass, Conner panted from their efforts while excitement sped the mink's breath. Already the exertion was getting to him and his tongue lolled, drops of saliva staining her camisole with each breath.

The front door slammed.

Both of them jumped. Conner lifted his head to find they were alone. The thought registered a blink before the screen door closed with a bang outside.

Conner started to lift off the couch before Beth caught his arm. "No, don't stop! Talk…later!" She pushed back against him. "Please."

Hesitation lasted for the length of one pant, long enough for her to clench down desperately.

Both hands went on her shoulders, pinning her under his weight as he shoved his hips. She squealed, and whether it was the rattle of his body crashing into hers or the pleasure of it, Beth vibrated under his palms. The first few seconds of her orgasm he thought she was trying to fight him off, but the rippling heat around him and her tight chirps kept him moving.

A thrill bolted through him. Was this what their game was all about? Pleasing her and feeling so powerful? No *wonder* they did this.

The spell broke when his knot struggled against her folds. Not sure if she could take it, he slowed and sat up. Beth twisted her upper body under him and came up, biting his chest, his neck, clutching at him.

Yelping, he shoved her away, holding her down, and only then did it occur that might be affection. She groaned and writhed under him. "I want it."

The first time the knot didn't catch, sliding out with effort and a pulled face from Beth, her eyes widening. The second time his knot caught and he shoved it as deep as it would go. His groan and lurching tugs were met with her gasping wriggles, and he emptied what felt like gallons into her until he couldn't breathe.

The dog fell back, panting hard. The exertion made his head dizzy, and he fumbled for the ice water, actually dragging her by their connection until his groping snagged it. With his nose in the glass, Conner drank hurriedly, an instant brain freeze screaming behind his eyes. Whatever her species did to keep from overheating, it was way more convenient than his.

Beth waited until he was finished before she leaned back and did the body twist thing again to hug his neck. Like a cat she somehow sprawled tonelessly, managing to coat his front with herself like she were liquid fur. Their kiss was soft and lazy, ending with him licking her muzzle. Each time he brushed her whiskers she giggled or twitched but let him.

The content silence stretched for several minutes until he asked, "Is turning like that uncomfortable at all?"

"Not really," she chirped, spent but chipper. "I can't sleep like this, but that's it."

Conner held her, running his fingers through sleek fur. "Did I do alright? I know you enjoyed that, but was the dominating part okay?"

Her eyes half-lidded. "Very pleasing, sir."

Muzzle wrinkling up, he said, "Do we need to keep doing that? When does it end?"

"Sorry, we can stop now." She rested her cheek on his throat and sighed. "I think you liked that too."

He nestled his face into her hair, nosed an ear, only to growl into it when she nipped his neck. "Oh yeah. Something I can get used to. What about you changed though? Tonight you've been comfortable in your own fur."

"Mmhm." She drew the sound out, rumbling her muzzle against his throat. "Being submissive, it gives me permission to do things that otherwise I'd rather hide under a bed than do. When the scene stops I get embarrassed and anxious again."

He hesitated before asking, "Do you like the stuff you do with Janine?

"It may be hard to believe, but yes." While she sounded honest, a sigh ruffled his throatfur. She sat up and propped an arm on his chest. "Things have been...tense lately, and she's not normally like this."

He bumped noses with her. "I'm surprised you didn't want to go after her."

Beth looked away, then hid her face on his chest. The bubble of contentment popped, drying up into the first uncomfortable silence he'd had with her.

It wasn't until his knot started to ease that she said, "There's lots of good reasons not to have done it. She would've been gone before we got out there. Chasing after her all hot and bothered would've made it worse. She should be given space. But...honestly, I didn't want to stop." Her sigh ruffled his fur, and her voice turned delicate. "Does that make me a bad person?"

Conner winced, but he squeezed her, and tucked his chin between her ears. "Thoughts or feelings aren't wrong, it's what we do about them that's important. We should've gone after her." He licked one of her little round ears. "All we can do is try to make it up to her, and try to not do it next time."

If there was a next time.

Beth looked down. "When will this thing let me go?"

"Need to get away from me that fast, huh? Lift up." With little more than a nudge he came loose, and she made a noise at the mess, but laid back down, facing him fully this time.

A thought bubbled up and made him tilt his head. "Shouldn't she have safeworded?"

"Yeah," Beth said. She looked distracted, but then her expression tightened. "She should've." The mink's whiskers flattened and her body tensed under him for a moment before she turned away. It was like the air pressure changed in the room.

Was it something he said? What did he do? He held back a whine, but it still scented his words. "What's wrong?"

"I'm sorry, just tired." The lie stuck out like a swollen lip, but he didn't call her on it.

Any bit of teasing or small talk was gently shut down. Something was up, but he didn't want to push. Partly, he was tired, but if she wasn't willing to talk with them so close like this, what else could he do?

After cleanup and a promise to see each other soon, he kissed her and went home.

* * *

While not hearing from Janine was expected, Conner was worried after the fourth day of Beth's silence. The hint had been received after the second unanswered text, the first ignored voicemail. Was this typical for her? Was the issue with him or Janine? Had Beth and Janine talked and fought?

Was keeping this relationship going even worth it? Before the first week was up he'd been hit with an avalanche of baggage and drama. Why was he putting up with this? The night at Beth's place had been great, and if it could work, he was very curious for more. It wasn't only the sex though that made him pause. Some issue was going on under the surface, not simply broken people but something that could be smoothed out, and he knew he could do it if he could get at it. Beth was so sweet and he wanted to see things work out.

On the fifth day he didn't know what to do. Calling her work was probably crossing some line, and he didn't want to dig the hole deeper. If this was how she handled conflict, he did need to know, because then he'd seriously let her know that this wasn't okay. There was someone who might have known, but he hadn't seen Janine outside of Beth's house, and now he saw that as a mistake.

With no other way of contacting her, Conner called the school's library. Thankfully someone other than Janine picked up. The librarian let him leave his name, number, and a request to "Please call me back when you can." That meant that Janine didn't need to call him during office hours, and might even choose to not call him at all. That way things could be okay, right? He wasn't sure if that was still unreasonable, or even if it was reasonable, if she'd still get upset.

For most of the day he was aware of his silent cellphone. By the early evening he had lost hope, and jerked in alarm at its ring.

"Is there something you want?" Janine asked in a tone that set Conner's tail against the back of his legs.

"Sorry. I didn't have any way to contact you," he said lamely. "But I need to talk about Beth."

She sighed through her nose. "There's nothing to talk about; she gets like this. Beth is an avoider."

"Well I'm not, and I don't think you are either. There are things you and I need to straighten out between us."

A moment of silence came on her end. Had he pushed too far?

"All right." For just a moment he thought that sounded pleased or maybe impressed. He breathed easier. "But I don't like talking on the phone."

Neither did he, so that worked out well.

* * *

They sat at the coffee shop's patio because the scent of all that ground coffee was too overwhelming for most canines. She arrived with arms folded and sat across from him like she had shown up to jury duty. It wasn't the death glare from the first time he'd met her, so he'd take it.

Conner took a deep breath. "You don't like sharing, I get that. Does that mean that you need to dislike me? Can you at least stop being all teeth?"

"I never growled at you once."

Conner pulled a face, digging fingers into his neckfur.

Her deep breath was more of a sigh. Ears lowered, she said, "I don't know. It's not personal."

That didn't make it any better, but neither would pointing that out. Rubbing his neck, he looked away too. "All of this is so new to me. I don't know what's acceptable with all this multiple partner leather stuff. Makes it hard to read the situation and know how to fix it. Can you tell me your problem specifically? Are you afraid of losing her, do you not want to deny something she wants, or is it just rude to say you don't want to share someone you love?"

"It's, well, I…goodness, you don't hold back the hard questions, do you?" Her shoulders hunched. "I can't tell her any of that. I have no place to because I never said anything about us. We never agreed on anything more than the 'leather stuff.'"

He sat forward. "Wait, you never told her how much you cared?"

Janine looked down.

"Never asked to be exclusive?"

She sighed.

"A couple?"

Janine said, "Not in those words, exactly. Or any words.

122

The day I was going to, she told me about you. Now it's too late, I've missed the opportunity.'"

Whoo boy. He shook his head. "You've gotta tell her. That could change everything. If you don't, and this goes forward as it is, things can definitely get worse."

"But what about you? You're involved here too, you could lose her."

He didn't buy that concern for a minute, it was a naked excuse. Instead of calling her on it, he told the truth. "She's nice, but I don't love her yet. You do."

"Even if you might not, you don't know if she feels the same. It's too late."

Conner spread his arms. "You're right, I don't know. Neither of us does. That's why you need talk to her."

The border collie's voice dropped too low. "What if she doesn't feel the same? If she wants to keep me at arm's length, especially after the other night? I've been fucking up right and left lately. What if she insists on a poly relationship? I don't know if I can swallow that."

He patted the back of her hand. "She likes you and she obviously wants to date *someone*. And I think she's pretty reasonable. Look, this is all 'what if', you can't do anything until you know 'what is'. I'll back you up if you want."

Eyes glistening, Janine smiled, and while he couldn't see from this angle, he knew her tail was wagging. "Thanks, really. You are being far too earnest and patient given how I've acted. You are disgustingly nice."

"If there's one thing to be disgusting about, I guess that's it." He grinned. "Let's make it better going forward. Oh, and something's been bugging me. Why didn't you safeword and talk? I asked Beth and she said you should've safeworded."

Janine sat back. "Ugh, I was upset and didn't think about it, didn't want to ruin your fun. Technically I wasn't part of the scene anyways, I was there monitoring to make sure everything was…"

Her gaze drifted off to the side, a thoughtful expression hanging for a moment before her muzzle scrunched up, ears hiking. "Oh shit."

Conner perked. "What?"

"How did Beth act after you asked her that?"

Tension started creeping into his shoulders. "Disinterested, pulling away, tired. Why?"

"No no no no," Janine chanted as she dug the phone out of her purse.

"Talk to me here."

She was already calling, finger up. They both sat in taut silence before Janine lowered the phone and sagged. "I was there to ensure safety. And I walked out right in the middle of it. You said you were a lifeguard? Imagine just leaving while there's a pool full of people."

Conner wilted. "Oh."

"Exactly." Janine dropped her muzzle. "But instead of random strangers in the pool, I was there for only one person. Now she doesn't trust me."

Conner shook his head and pushed his chair back, standing. "We don't know that, not until we talk to her. If she won't answer the phone…will she answer the door?"

* * *

Evening's low light had robbed the tiny porch of any cheerful warmth. Walking up, Conner could feel a chill running up his spine. Janine's tail hung low beside him as they stepped up to the door. He had to do something, though. Ignoring the possibilities that rushed through his head, Conner knew that Janine wouldn't be the one to make the first move. For her, he had to do this. Getting to the door, he gave a smile and knocked.

Above them the porch light flushed on. "Who is it?"

Conner said, "We came over to see you."

Opening the door half way, the mink sidled in the gap. Normally Conner found it cute and sexy when women wore too-big shirts like nightgowns, but at that moment she looked fragile and exposed. Beth kept her eyes on the welcome mat. "I've got a lot of work to do, get handouts ready, set lesson plans—"

Janine said, "I can see the book you were reading from here." Conner certainly couldn't, not from this angle, and he doubted the other dog's eyes were better than his.

The bluff worked though, Beth's whiskers spreading as her brow crinkled. "I'm not in a social mood right now, okay?"

"We're not here to hang out, we're worried." Conner leaned in, bumping his nose against her forehead. "There's stuff we want to tell you."

She stepped back, giving them room to come in, but crossed her arms without welcome. Fur starting to fluff up in something like annoyance. She said, "You too? Are we going to have this 'serious relationship talk' every time we have a disagreement?" The words had an edge.

"If you hide every time we do," Janine said.

A fierceness flashed in Beth's eyes. "Maybe I'm hiding because there are things I shouldn't say to you that I haven't stopped wanting to say yet." She couldn't hold the glare though, her eyes dipping to the carpet. "And it's especially difficult to talk to you like two people, because every time I look at you I start backsliding into subservience. That's weird and probably not a good sign."

Conner squeezed her shoulders. "It's hard, but we'll listen. I'll back you up if you need me."

"Okay. Can I get you anything to dri—" she stopped and pulled a face. "There I go again. You know where the kitchen is." She pulled away, her movements fast and tight. Conner looked to Janine, and the other dog had went stiff and alert, ears sideways. This wasn't usual.

The mink took the far end of the couch, and Janine followed, claiming her usual chair. That left Conner with Beth's usual seat, the middle ground. Probably fitting.

Turning to Janine, Conner said, "We need to hear her out, so she needs to go first until she's finished." If Janine apologized or confessed before Beth, he had a feeling it could come across as simply trying to be manipulative and shut the argument down.

The other dog's muzzle scrunched up like she wanted to protest, but she nodded. "Alright. What're you upset about?"

Beth's legs disappeared under her shirt as she drew them up to her chest and hugged them. "First, when I tried to tell you about Conner, you wouldn't even let me because of your rules. Then when I could tell you, you laid down rules, more hoops to jump through. When I jumped through those, then more hoops showed up, ones he and I had to jump through, and then—"

"He asked me to teach him."

"He asked *us*." Beth's fur bristled. She rubbed her face, then simply covered her eyes and rested the elbow on the couch's arm. "I gave you an out, I offered to do it alone, and you volunteered. You volunteered to make sure everything was okay, and then you ditched that. You didn't follow your own rules.

The collie's ears went down and back. "This is all about rules, are you saying you don't want them anymore?"

"I'm saying things are so rigid, you're so demanding, your standards are so high, I never get an inch, but where are the rules for you? Who holds you to them?"

Janine's muzzle opened, then closed. "What do you want?"

"To not be abandoned, for one."

Conner leaned forward. "Hey." He needed to steer things from escalating. "Do you really feel like she left you?"

The mink had an inkling of a glare before it faltered. She glanced down at her knees. "No, that was just frustration. I don't feel betrayed or unsafe. But I don't like where it points, what it could lead to."

Silence settled in. After a moment, Janine said, "You're supposed to tell me how you feel in emails. You haven't."

The heat leaked from Beth's tone. "Yeah well, I don't know if you'll bristle, or how well you'll listen anymore." Glancing at him she said, "As long as I'm supposed to be gushing my feelings, Conner, I actually kinda didn't want you to get involved in the whole kinky stuff."

Conner cocked his head. "But when I asked, you said yes."

"Yeah." She hid her eyes again. "I was so caught up in you being so okay with everything that I didn't really think about it until after everything blew up. The other night was great, don't get me wrong, but I was looking for with a partner was…down time with someone. Snuggling, going out. Being a couple."

Janine's ears splayed.

After a deep breath, Beth said, "I think that's everything. What's going on with you?"

For the first time since he'd met her, Janine looked lost and scared, not just the nervousness of when they arrived. She glanced to Conner and he nodded.

"I'm sorry I didn't listen to you, and I'm sorry I left. The other night I was upset, and I've stayed upset, because it's hard to see you with someone else because I love you. You being with him is what I want for us and that tears me up."

Beth stared first at Janine and then into space. Finally she turned to Conner. "You're good at this, what do you think? I'm afraid this will make me sound awful, but this feels really convenient. I don't know what to think."

He winced, and couldn't bring himself to look at Janine. "I think she's being totally honest and what you just did was probably why she didn't say anything. Because she was working up the nerve to tell you when you told her about me."

Covering her face with a hand, Beth sucked air through her teeth.

He let that sink in before adding, "And if she'd asked to be together when you brought me up, that might've looked just as manipulative."

Beth took a minute to chew on that. "Hold on a minute. Whose idea was it to tell me? Did you push her?"

"Yes, why?"

"Because it's been killing her and she was going to keep it bottled up." Beth turned concerned eyes on Janine. "You were up front about not liking this, but you were doing it for me. Okay, thank you. But this is serious, it was causing you real pain, and it's been making you…unpleasant, and you left a scene you were monitoring. You were going to keep hiding this, and it would've hurt all of us."

"I couldn't tell you because I didn't want to lose you!" Janine growled, "You wanted something else, and I thought I couldn't give it to you because I don't have a prick, so I held to anything I could. By the way It's fucking rich-

"Janine—"

"—being lectured about hiding feelings when we had to storm your door to get you to talk."

"Stop!" He could put enough power in his voice without shouting. Both women hesitated. "None of us are happy about what we did, but it's already happened. All we can do is agree it was wrong and do it differently from now on. We have to see where we go from here. Beth, do you trust Janine?"

Beth looked at Janine and nodded.

"Do you want to be together with her?"

She took a breath. "Yes."

Closing her eyes, Janine's ears raised for the first time.

Conner said, "If she decides she can't share you with me, if you have to choose, can you choose her?"

"Yes." Beth smiled. "Sorry."

Janine looked between him and the mink.

"Janine, now that you know I'm not coming between you two, can you deal with this?"

She shook her head. "I don't know. Right now I'm up, I'm down, my door has never been open for men but I could kiss you right now for cutting through all of this. Things may be different in a month or two, but no promises."

"Okay." He sighed, breathing easier now that the air was clear. "I can respect that, and if this isn't working out, then I'll step out. But you have to tell me. You two like rules, well here's a relationship rule: we have to talk. No more hiding. Right?"

Janine said, "Alright."

"Okay." Beth's whiskers fanned out. "If we're making rules and establishing things, then...Janine, I can't do a 24/7 kink relationship. There has to be downtime. Even if it's just you and me."

Janine nodded. "I see that. It's not for everyone and I hadn't realized how much you were struggling."

"One last thing." He pursed his lips. "This will suck but I suggest no sex stuff for a couple of weeks. Let's hang out and see how we are together, without that complication?"

Neither looked pleased, but they grumbled an agreement.

"Cool." His tail wagged. "Now this is cheesy, but everybody hug it out. C'mon."

The two women came together first and Conner gave them a few seconds. The mink pressed her nose into the dog's throat, and Janine hugged her tight. He put his arms around Beth from behind, and the other dog squeezed his shoulder.

Small victories.

Beth nipped Conner's jaw. "I hadn't thought that poly would lead to getting ganged up on."

"We just needed to find some common ground, I guess." Janine shot him a smile.

Pulling back, Conner clapped his hands. "I think we all feel like we had a hard workout. I'm a firm believer in the best remedy for scrapes and bruises is ice cream."

Janine looked to Beth. "He might just be a keeper."

THREE TO TANGO

The trill of a phone pulled Amadi out of a doze. Springing off the couch, the serval stalked the wily cell down and answered. "Hello?"

"Hey. Where are you?" Marjani said, the cheer in her voice surprising him.

Fighting an urge to yawn, he padded back to the couch. "Home." He snatched up the remote and turned off the TV.

"How much of a disaster is the house in?"

Amadi glanced around the living room: a day-old pizza box, a half-eaten bag of chips in the recliner, his work shoes kicked off in random directions. Clothes lay where he'd shed them and he knew used dishes sat on the kitchen counter. "I'm keeping it clean." The serval could only get away with it when she wasn't around, so he had to cash in all of his laziness when the opportunity presented itself.

"I'm sure. Listen, do you remember where the cellphone headset is?"

"Uhh…."

Marjani sighed. "Go look in the office closet."

Amadi flicked his tail. "Alright. Hold on." He set the phone down. Having learned it was easier to not ask why, he prowled into the office and combed through packets of printer paper, empty boxes of things still under warranty, power strips—ah! He pulled the headset out from beneath an extra USB cable, causing a small electronics avalanche. Once he'd replaced everything, the serval reclaimed the phone. "Got it." Amadi dropped onto the couch and set the headset on the coffee table.

"Good. Argh, I have another call. I'll call you right back." She hung up.

Poor Jani. Some days she'd been so tired she couldn't call him, and others she was too frustrated to talk without venting, a no-no in a condo with someone always in earshot. Amadi missed her, and losing their anniversary sucked.

He answered the phone on the first ring this time. "Okay," she said, "sorry about that." Was that excitement he heard?

"How are you? You sound good. They finally let you get away?"

Marjani said, "I had to leave before I started clawing something. Told mom I was going to see a movie and then work on freelance at a coffee shop."

"Oh, what are you going to go see?"

"Not a thing." The quality of Marjani's voice changed, like she had switched to speakerphone. "I'm parked in a nice secluded spot so we can have phone sex."

"Ooh." Well. He smiled. "What happens if I don't want to?"

"Then I'll find a way to strangle you with my mind, because I really need this."

The serval laughed. "Is that what the headset's for?"

Her voice dropped into a purr. "You will be holding more important things. Plug the headset in."

The adapter didn't want to go in at first but he finally slotted it into place. He tucked in the earbud and adjusted the mouth piece so it fit the length of his muzzle. "How do I sound?"

"Good. Now…I didn't bother with a bra, and my sweats are in the back seat, so all I have on is a tight shirt and some red lace tangas."

"Nice." He doubted she'd taken pretty underwear on her trip but he appreciated the mental image.

"What about you?"

Amadi glanced down at the oversized hockey jersey draped over his otherwise naked body. She gave him a hard time whenever he wore "that tattered old rag," the fabric thin enough to show the buttery color of his fur and in other places tiny holes had crept into the fraying material, but he had nothing more comfortable and the memories of college made him love it too much. "A gimp mask and high heels."

A knock at the door swiveled his ears and distracted him from her laughter. "Hold on, someone's here." Should he put something else on? Nah, he didn't need pants. The jersey hung to his upper thighs like a dress. Whoever it was might get a peek at his nuts, but that was the price for disturbing him this late at night.

He pulled the front door open a foot and peered through. "Hello?"

Amadi's eyes had yet to adjust from the bright interior to the dark porch, leaving him only able to pick out a female something shorter than him in a beige uniform, a hat over her eyes.

The female said, "I'm here about a delivery."

"Jani, did you order something?" He opened the door wider and stepped out.

Marjani chuckled. "She's actually there to pick up a package."

The delivery girl snagged the hem of his jersey and pulled it up. With her other hand she cupped his balls.

Amadi yowled and leaped back into the house, nearly tumbling onto his ass.

She stepped inside and closed the door. Now he had a better look at the nut-brown squirrel; she wore tiny khaki shorts with a matching button-down shirt and hat. Brunette curls bounced against her shoulders. She planted a hand on her hip and grinned with buckteeth. "There's no delivery, but

I definitely have a box you'll be interested in."

"Remember the train thing?" Marjani sounded just a hint sheepish. After a day of being pissed, he'd gotten over it, but he still planned on not letting her forget it. "Kahlua here is going to help me make up for it. Happy belated anniversary?"

A wholly feline smile snuck across his muzzle. "This just might make us square."

Looking at her fully, Amadi realized she wasn't a squirrel—her tail, a foot too short and not quite as bushy, had bands of black and white running up it like racing stripes, while more white circled her honey brown eyes. Where squirrels were lanky, Kahlua's frame sported curvy hips, a subtle outward curve to her belly, and a full rack she was busy exposing button-by-button. When she noticed him eyeing her Kahluah's chubby cheeks dimpled in a lecherous smile. A chipmunk, definitely.

"So. I'm all yours tonight." Opening her shirt, the chipmunk brushed her fingers over the paunch of her stomach and up the sides of her breasts. "Where do you want to start?"

"With those delicious tits." Amadi grinned back, all teeth.

Marjani said, "I thought you might approve."

Giggling, Kahlua walked past him into the living room, putting an extra bounce and sway into her hips. The serval happily followed that round, perky ass. So focused was he on how her shorts desperately held her curves that he nearly knocked her over when she stopped by the couch. She surveyed the room with a sigh that said, "Men," before turning back to him.

Reaching out to her chest, Amadi had only a moment to caress the soft fur around an areola before Kahlua grabbed the front of his jersey and shoved him onto the couch. Planting a sneaker between his knees, the chipmunk smirked down at him. "Lose the shirt." The jersey ended up across the TV.

She took a moment to leer over his spotty frame before

straddling his lap and shoving her chest into his face. Obliging her, Amadi nuzzled into her cleavage, dolling out a few licks as he cupped one tit, taunting the lovely nipple. Normally he was far more keen on butts than breasts, but compared to his wife the chipmunk had more of everything, making for a nice change of pace. "Jani, where did you find this girl?" he rumbled, partially muffled.

"Internet," Kahlua chittered into his ear.

In his other ear his wife replied, "We've been talking for the last two weeks. Had to properly vet her."

"Mmhm," Amadi added while nosing at one of Kahlua's nipples; it was fat and brown and for all the world reminded him of acorn tops. He licked over it, first focusing his tongue's raspy roughness, then pressed in with his piercing to tickle her nipple's tip. Groaning with enthusiasm the chipmunk arched her back, smothering his face with warm furred flesh. Suckling on her nub earned him an ear rubbing.

Instead of playing with his now quite-ready-erection, Kahlua lifted herself up and nudged his cock underneath her, then sat on it, pinning him under a cheek. His grunt of disappointment came out deeper when her weight shifted, putting lovely amounts of pressure on his prick before she started to wiggle.

"She certainly teases like you," Amadi grumbled before wrapping his teeth around Kahlua's nipple, taunting it as he sucked.

Both women laughed, Kahlua's a chirry giggle and Marjani's a more smoky delight. "She can't tease all the time," Marjani said, "like when she pulls a train. Said she likes three or four guys lined up behind her raring to go, grabbing her and pinning her one at a time until she's a drippy mess. She likes come all in her fur."

Probably Marjani made that up for the sake of teasing him. Which was fine; he loved her lewd little stories and details, and with the chipmunk in his lap he could just imagine her at the head of a cock queue, thighs spread and urging them forwards. Amadi let go of her teat, lifted his muzzle to her shoulder, and bit hard enough to let her know he liked to use his teeth.

She gasped, pulling away, then grinned and shoved him back. "Careful there, putty tat. You'll get me all excited."

"I already have."

The pressure increased on his dick before she lifted her weight and hip-shimmied, the motion whisking her shorts over his taut hard-on. "I can tell. How about we do something about that?" When he growled in approval Kahlua slid off his lap and onto her knees.

"The missus suggested that I do some things she either didn't care for, or wasn't 'equipped' to pull off." Scooping up her breasts and parting them, the chipmunk leaned in until his cock slotted between them, then she smooshed her breasts closed. With her resting her rack on his lap, only his cock-tip escaped the fluff of her cleavage. "She said something about buttfucking?"

Well.

Kahlua's eyes sparkled under her hat's brim, her dangling curls framing dimples.

"Jani, have I told you how much of a good woman you are?"

"Not often enough," she purred. "What is she doing?"

"We're abou- rrwl," he stuttered as the chipmunk's tongue swirled over his glans. "about to titfuck."

Marjani mm'd. "Sounds fun," she said, before her breath caught. "I'm starting, too. Just a finger right now. I've not taken my underwear off yet."

Capturing his tip in her muzzle, Kahlua sucked until her cheeks dented. Her head rolled about a moment before jerking back with a wet pop. With a little bounce, she began to lift her shoulders, the warm fur of her cleavage caressing him in a silky embrace. She cupped her breasts and squeezed them together, tightening all around his shaft. "When I'm riding a guy reverse cowgirl, I like to pull out and do this with my ass until I feel a hot load splash my tail and drip down my cheeks, let it seep into the fur. Makes an impression after anal, don't you think?"

"Oh, you talk dirty too?" Well. He believed her about as much as his wife's claims, but points for the effort.

Marjani said, "I gave her some pointers."

A series of dings dragged Amadi's eyes from the chipmunk's cleavage. "I sent you some pictures." Amadi reached around Kahlua and snatched up the phone, scrolling through the explicit snapshots of Marjani displayed up against a window, her pussy dripping. He could see a guy's dark furred leg in there, but the focus was not his wife's partner.

"There were pictures and I'm only now getting them?"

Unable to help himself, Amadi started to thrust, clapping his lap against the underside of Kahlua's rack. "Ooh, those pictures are hot, aren't they?" she cooed and relaxed, the serval doing the work as she teased his crown with warm, enthusiastic affection.

"Stop whining, you've got them don't you?" Marjani's pout was audible. "You should be more delighted."

Kahlua pinned his thighs to the couch with her palms as her lips wrapped around his glans. Rather than suck, she left her lips loose and dragged them around his tip, flirting them at the base before drawing them up to just kiss his slit. Every now and then the chipmunk blew out, forcing the air to tickle past his head and down his shaft. The sassy thing actually rubbed the front of her buck teeth across his tip.

"Uhff, how many pointers did you give her?" Frustrated need growled through his teeth. "She uses her mouth too fucking light, just like you."

His wife laughed, her voice tight. "That's all her, I'm afraid. Mmm, I could use your cock in my mouth right now." Her breath hissed quick into the phone. "I'm getting close…."

By the sound of Marjani's panting in his ear, her vibrator was out and she was racing him. " Come on her face Amadi. Come on her face and send me the pictures."

"Working on it," he groaned back.

The teasing ended with a quick, wicked suction; the chipmunk pinching down with her lips, tugging repeatedly. Pulling free with a wet pop and a gasp, she lifted her head and chest, and started pumping her breasts around his dick.

An eager pressure was building, pressing up against his insides. Part warning and partly for Marjani's benefit, he grunted, "I'm gonna—"

"Do it," Kahlua cut him off, making wicked eye contact as she sped up her bouncing. She pressed her breasts together harder, the friction of fur on skin almost painful. Closing her eyes, she chirred, "Hit me with it."

The first shot tagged her under the chin. Amadi flexed his kegels, spurting harder with an accompanying yowl. When he was done purring and staring into space, Amadi surveyed the damage. Somewhere in there Kahlua had raised her chest, partially burying his tip in her cleavage; while a rope or two striped the underside of her muzzle, his mess had mostly pooled up around the "V" of her chest, along the inner curves, and a few fat drops had dribbled over her throat.

Amadi tipped over on his side, half-curling and flicking his tail, his purr a steady burble. "She's a real mess," he said for his wife's benefit.

The chipmunk laughed. "I take it you're satisfied. Don't forget the pictures," she added, and passed him the phone.

Marjani came in his ear before he took the first pic, and he worked the camera through the serenade with a smile. After the first two, Kahlua rubbed his come into her fur, then posed and licked her fingers while making eyes with the camera.

"You can clean up if you want." He finished, sending Jani one of the better ones.

She sighed and stretched, then bounced to her feet. "Thanks, I don't want you drying in my fur. But don't get comfortable, we're not done by a long shot, sweetspots."

"I'm glad I brought some moist towelettes." The relaxed haze in Marjani's voice brought a smile to Amadi's muzzle.

Amadi said, "I'm really enjoying this anniversary, but I feel bad you're all alone. Maybe a cop will spot your car and he can join in."

"Don't even joke about that!" Marjani laughed.

Kahlua poked her head out of the kitchen. "Hey handsome, where's your lube?"

"I'll get it." A thought gave him pause as he rooted through the dresser's sex drawer. "So what did you do when the train stopped?"

Marjani said, "We sat very, very still, and when everyone who was leaving shuffled off, we fled to the bathroom."

"Together?" Ah-ha, the bottle was hiding under a blindfold.

Marjani scoffed. "No. We didn't do anything else after that. I did kiss him goodbye at his stop but that was it. I said no to giving him my number, but I think he was happy enough."

Back in the living room he dropped onto the couch. "And whoever picked you up didn't notice your just-fucked glow or the smell?"

"Told her I sat next to a skunk the whole way, and his natural scent covered everything else, I think. The rest was just exhaustion and being all roughed up from the travel. Thankfully she didn't want to ask questions."

Kahlua strutted back to him. When he looked up, she

unbuttoned her shorts, peeling the zipper down. Turning, she paffed him in the face with her tail, swaying it under his chin. He made a grab for her tail, but she hiked it as she tilted her hips. Down the shorts went, showing off how the bell of her hips made for broad, round cheeks. She'd skipped underwear. Amadi would have complained, but the thought evaporated when Kahlua cupped one of her cheeks and spread them only to send a finger drifting down the crease. "Ready for round two?"

Amadi glanced down. "Uh...not exactly."

"That works out perfectly." She stepped out of her stripped shorts, leaving only her open shirt, hat and shoes. The chipmunk draped herself over his lap, grabbing one of the throw pillows and propping her chin on it. "Be a gentleman and lube me up."

Whump! His first spank sent a jiggle through the plush curves. He snatched the base of her tail, yanked up, and spanked her now hiked ass and thighs. She chirped and glanced back at him before the brush of her tail obscured the view. Once he earned enough squeaks to satisfy him, the cat ran his fingers over her abused spots, the fur ruffled and askew in places. When she wiggled in approval, the serval caressed with clawtips, turning her shiver into a tremble.

"You finished?" All the amusement in her voice ruined the mock indignation she put out.

His fingertips tickled across her damp folds. "Just about," he said and sank two digits inside her pussy.

Marjani rumbled in his ear, "Ooh, I could hear that moan. What're you doing?"

"She's really sensitive," he replied as Kahlua's insides rippled around his fingers. "Getting her ready before I slide under her tail." Moving his fingers in steady but lazy motions, Amadi stirred about, then pulled free to delicately pinch and tug on one of her slick lips. Kahlua squirmed for him, hugging the pillow tight, and squeezed his wrist with her thighs. *My turn to tease*, he thought as he tapped out a tune on her clit. "I'm fingering her, but I'm thinking of you."

"Tsk tsk," his wife chided. "That's sweet, but, no you're not, and I've started again anyways. You should be more concerned with making her feel like she's your focus."

Amadi said, "So Kahlua, you're really down for anal?"

"Mmhm." She arched her hips and squeezed his fingers. "I have the most intense orgasms from it if I've already came."

Amadi cupped the chipmunk's mound and worked his wrist in tight circles. "Hear that, Jani? Anal gives her really intense orgasms."

"Well, I'm very happy for her," Marjani said dryly.

Chuckling, Amadi went back to an aggressive fingering. When he didn't stop after minute, Kahlua glanced back, her breath starting to rise. "Are you gonna get me ready?"

"Well, you said it's intense after your first orgasm." His fingers went back to her nub and worked it like an intense videogame's buttons. "That means you have to get off first."

Her tense sigh was delighted. "Oh you are such a clever kitty."

The focused attention unwound her quickly. Each gasp went higher until she came with a stuttering, adorable squeak. Clearly not a big release for her, but the night was still young.

Amadi trailed his moist digits up to taunt her ring, carefully strumming a claw along the wrinkled skin. Beneath him she twitched, her tail stuttering in his grasp, and finally she squeaked as the tip of his finger pushed inside. Lube would come but her wetness provided just enough slickness to tease. Amadi swirled his fingertip, then sank up to his first knuckle and curled his finger, stretching her further. When he started tugging that curled up finger, Amadi grinned at the unlady-like sounds he milked out of her.

He withdrew and began the real prep. Despite all the talk

of how she adored an ass-fucking, she felt tight—but then, Amadi hadn't had many experiences he could compare her against.

Once she was properly lubed, he tossed all coy pretenses out and drove two slick fingers into her aggressively enough to thump his fist against her butt. Kahlua arched her back, the motion bumping her belly against his stiff tip.

Oh, he was finally hard again. He'd been far too intent on his task to notice. Well.

"I think I'm ready," she said and squeezed down on his fingers, her voice thick with wanting more.

"Just in time, my arm is starting to get tired."

One more dollop and he was satisfied. She climbed off his lap and, as he started lubing himself up, too, she stepped over to bend across the couch's end. "No, not there—follow me." Doing it there would put her hips higher than her head and while great for pussy, he wanted better leverage for this. It might also end in a mess on the couch. He led Kahlua into the kitchen and knocked on the table. After a moment's consideration, he shoved a few things out of the way.

With a smirk, the chipmunk leaned in and spoke into his headset, "He's so chivalrous." That got a laugh out of Marjani. Kahlua flashed a bucktoothed grin, then turned and bent over the table, her tail straightening like an eager exclamation point.

"Brat," he accused with a grin and slapped her once, twice across the ass.

Kahlua gasped. "You know it." She wiggled her hips and hiked her tail. "Like my butt, huh?"

"Oh yeah. In fact, I'm about to get really into it."

She swatted him with her tail. "Oh that's awful." Reaching back, she cupped her cheeks and spread wide. "Come on in."

The serval stepped up and slid his wet tip down her ass's hot groove to nudge her ring. A hiss escaped her as his glans sank inside and he pressed deeper. Slow and careful—an inch in, an inch back, two in and one back—just like the how-to guide said. Finally Amadi snuggled up to the chipmunk's cushioned butt with a tense sigh that she echoed. "I'm balls deep, honey."

Marjani let loose a tight breath and mm'd, "Fuck her extra hard for me."

"I'm not doing it for you." He let them both get used to this, lazily rocking back and swinging home again.

Kahlua lifted up on her hands and pushed back, the two meeting with a grinding roll that bared Amadi's teeth. He briefly caught her peeking around her tail before she squeezed, coaxing an arched back and a growl out of him. Clutching her cheeks hard enough to prick her even with his claws sheathed, the serval pulled back and shoved once, twice, three times, his crotch clapping against her thighs.

The moan he earned pushed him further, but he eased the enthusiasm back to a smoother, longer thrusting which lacked that wicked collision. Kahlua reached underneath her and he felt the shiver and ripple of her insides, so she was probably playing with herself.

She chittered, "You wanna come in me or on me?"

The thought sped him up. "Don't know, hff, yet."

Beneath him, the chipmunk curled her back and he found her hand wrapped around his nuts. "Don't be coy," she chirped, squeezing him. "However you're going to do it… give it to me hard and now."

Amadi growled, but only after she released his balls. So, that's how the sassy little slut wanted to play? Brushing aside her bushy tail he reached down, sank his fingers into the bountiful curls spilling out of her hat and dragged her into a taut arch by her hair. When she squealed in surprise, he merely bared his fangs and slammed into her hard enough for the table to scrape across the floor. Kahlua chirped and clutched the table's edge, her breaths already tight and high.

Their fucking made a terrible racket until the table was jammed against the wall, letting him smash his lap against her plush ass with impunity, replacing the noise with the slap of eager bodies. She widened her stance and shoved back, her shoes squeaking across the linoleum in protest. With her legs spread, his balls kept a secondary drumbeat against her wet cunt, occasionally bumping her frantic fingers.

The chipmunk went off like a squeaking fire alarm. The walls around him tightened so wickedly, and he could dully feel her pussy's fluttering. As much as it pained him, Amadi stopped moving, letting her feel full as she went over. His resolve to be still ended before she relaxed, though, his pace picking up in a hurry.

Kahlua pulled her arm from beneath her and sagged. For the first time, she had no bratty comeback; had he actually fucked her into silence?

Leaning over to brace a hand on her shoulder, Amadi put his back into pounding out his need before bursting inside of her with a breathless hiss. Dimly, he noticed the chipunk's tail fluttering against his chest as she squirmed, squeezing down on his pulsing dick. The cat sagged over her, breathing hard, and gave her ears a few nuzzles, whiskers tickling across their edges.

Kahlua sprawled on the table, boneless and content. He draped over her, drunk on the rich scent of sex hanging in the room.

The warm glow was beginning to clear when he heard Marjani go off, and he took the time to listen before rising and easing free of the chipmunk. A glance at the table reminded him of the way it had scooted and banged the wall; Jani would kill him if the wall or floor were scratched.

"Where do you think you're going?" Kahlua's sated voice didn't match the wickedness in her expression. "We've got all night, sweetspots."

He chuckled. "Jani, I'm going to have to do something to thank you when you get back."

"Mmhm," she said with a languid purr. "What do you think of a train ride?"

TLC

"Hold still," Margaret said, leaning over her husband before taking hold of the sheet that had come off the adjustable bed's corner. "Rise up a little." Planting a hand by his head to steady herself, she gave several tugs before tucking it back behind the mattress. "This set of sheets is always so stubborn, the elastic must be poor." It would have been easier had they not tucked the bed against the wall, but Henry preferred the view. Finally she managed to get the corner to behave.

"There," she concluded and sat back beside him. A slight, sly smile peeked at the edges of his muzzle, and she almost asked what he was thinking when her tail, swishing to drape over his lap, brushed against something rigid. Margaret glanced down to see him tenting the sheet.

She peered at the other fox. "Were you staring down my shirt?"

That smile deepened. "Where was I supposed to look? They were practically on my nose."

"Lecher," she said with a feigned tsking. Well, she might as well take care of his erection.

Margaret tossed the sheet covering him aside, exposing his penis. Unless the physical therapist was coming or he was leaving the house, they didn't bother with dressing his lower half anymore; it just got in the way. She took his penis in hand and began pumping. Just one of several new duties she had to do, now that the strength in his arms was going; it had surprised her just how much effort needed to go into masturbating him, as Henry could sometimes take fifteen minutes to finish.

Not that she couldn't handle the affair. Just like scrubbing dishes the old fashioned way, or getting a particularly stubborn stain out of the carpet. Which is how she thought of tending to this. At first it had been embarrassing, but she just went to stroking with her efficient persistence. Margaret almost started humming, a habit when her hands worked at a chore.

"Margaret."

With her free hand she absently stroked his thigh, and then moved to where his knot should be rising. Was this going to be another one of those fifteen minute processes?

"Margaret!"

"Hm?" She glanced away from the window and caught him with an odd expression, his ears half back. It didn't slow her hand down.

He touched her wrist. "You don't …need to do that."

The vixen tilted her head. "Something wrong?"

A knock at the front door perked both their ears. Henry leaned towards the window. "Looks like the nurse."

"She's an hour early," Margaret said with a frown and covered him back up. The sheet was far too thin for that to hide him. "Drape your…" She almost said tail, but remembered the difficulty of wrestling it from where it dangled through a slot in the bed, now as limp as his legs.

"Just go, I'm not exactly new at dealing with this."

Margaret shook her head as she passed into the hall. The disease sure hadn't slowed down his libido. She expected him to grin and leer at her up until-

A realization stabbed into her so swiftly she had to check her voice in the foyer. "Coming!" A barbed thought ran rampant inside her and she fought to make her face acceptable, to bring her ears up.

When she thought she was presentable, Margaret opened

the door. "Sorry about that."

"It's okay." The rabbit shouldered her bag and stepped in past her, her attentive eyes moving towards the bedroom.

"He's waiting for you," Margaret said with a smile that lasted only as long as Rachel stayed in view.

Ignoring the sounds of the other two talking, the vixen padded through the kitchen, closed the pantry door, and only then allowed herself to cry.

Soon they wouldn't be able to make love. At least, she doubted *she* could.

The doctors had said it would be beneficial to continue making love, as many couples did as the condition progressed. They had sex about once a month; it was uncommon for her mood and his physical energy to mesh. Still, poor Henry needed all the relaxation and momentary enjoyment she could give him, and now a guilty pang dug into her for not doing more.

Yet when his arms finally did go, Henry would lie there, unable to even touch her, and Margaret didn't think she could bear to do it then, like she would be molesting some mannequin. Just thinking that sent a wash of guilt through her. Even if his arms could work, his lungs might not be able to handle the exertion much longer, either. Up until now she hadn't thought about sex once the rest of his body went.

She wasn't some nymphomaniac desperate for sex, but the thought of losing yet another part of their lives cut into her.

The phone rang, but she ignored it, instead working to compose herself. Rachel wouldn't be terribly long, and the vixen could find a more convenient time to be hysterical. Once calmed down enough, she went in search of the phone.

Alex had called. She dialed him back. "Mom," he said as soon as he picked up, "I can't come tonight. I'm being forced to pull mandatory overtime."

"But you have to! I can't get him into the chair on my own anymore." Or from the chair into the car for that matter. "He's been looking forward to this ball game, they play the rival team only once, twice a year. You've already been promising to take him to the movies for two weeks."

"I know, I know. I'm behind the eight ball here. Can you see if Sam can do it tonight?"

Watching Samantha's little ones, on top of everything else, was the last thing Margaret needed right now. Her disappointment in Alex leaked past her lips. "I will try. We'll do what we can."

"I'm sorry. I have to get back to work."

By the time she finished ironing out the logistics with Samantha, Rachel came looking for her. Margaret set the phone down and perked up, tight with the threat of bad news. "How is he?"

"Well…His breathing and talking look good, motor skills in his fingers are great."

The vixen nodded. "He works very hard on those with the physical therapist, and he's always on the laptop. Did he mention he's started getting too much spit?"

Rachel said, "He doesn't have more saliva so much as starting to have trouble swallowing what he normally has."

A little sigh escaped Margaret. "He's not mentioned any problems swallowing to me. Eating seems fine."

"It may not be very noticeable right now, but it will soon." Rachel hesitated, buck teeth worrying her lower lip. "The biggest problem is I think the medication's not helping anymore."

Margaret crumpled inside. ALS killed inch by inch, and nothing could stop it, making treatment all about delaying the inevitable. Once it set into wearing down his lungs….Her voice wrung dry of hope. "How long?"

The rabbit's floppy ears flipped when she shook her head.

"I'm not a doctor—"

"But you've been seeing him for months, you must have some idea."

Rachel settled a hand on Margaret's forearm. "My best guess, and this is just a guess, is that he has six, seven months. You really should go back to the doctor for more tests."

She let Rachel go with a numb "Thank you," and stood in the kitchen, out of tears and back to the grinding daily grieving they lived with now. Seven months. He wouldn't even make it to fifty five.

After checking to see if Henry needed anything, Margaret lay down to rest before Samantha showed up. Despite the weary exhaustion saddled on her, she couldn't fall asleep. One worry tumbled into the next. Eventually it rolled back to her fears for their lovemaking. If the once-a-month routine continued, their bodies might say goodbye once, maybe twice more before his arms went completely.

Well then, she had to make sure sex happened more than that. They both deserved it, but she needed to make more of an effort for him, too. Being adventurous and salacious had always been something Margaret failed at. Even the passing of her parents hadn't helped her shake their strict and tight-lipped upbringing. One compromise she found easy to make was wearing clothes to bed – heels, sexy underthings, sometimes whole outfits. Ideas started to percolate.

The front door opened after a single announcing knock. Samantha had never been one to respect things like closed doors, and her little troop of a family crashed in like a carnival. Margaret got up to meet the chaos.

Soon Henry sat in his chair, talking with Samantha's husband, Seya, while the grandkits interrupted him with excited questions or chewing on his coat. She watched from the kitchen doorway.

"What's wrong?"

Margaret started. Samantha had snuck up on her after coming from the bathroom. "Nothing's wrong."

"I know better. You're chomping ice." When Margaret gave her a dubious look, the younger vixen shrugged her shoulders. "Remember that stuffed bee Alex took everywhere? When dad ran over it with the lawnmower, you were chewing ice before you broke the news to Alex. You were chewing ice that whole month you and dad separated. And then—"

"I guess it helps relieve stress," Margeret murmured, popping a cube in her mouth.

Samantha quieted. "Is it about dad?"

Instead of answering, she chewed.

"I had a feeling… You look rough."

The girl should have been a detective. Or did Margaret just look that bad? "Could you remind Alex to come by? I don't want to keep asking him. You know how the more I push, the more he pushes back."

"Like he'll listen to me? But sure." They watched Henry with the grandkids. Over his shoulder, Seya looked at Samantha and pointed at his watch. Quickly she said, "Mom, would you like to go to a spa?"

"A spa? We don't have the mon—"

Samantha shook her head. "One of the moms at scouts, she works at a spa. I could try to get some kind've discount from her."

"But your father—"

"Dad! Have you been birding lately?"

Henry looked back before grumping, "Not in a while, no."

Quieter, she said, "He needs to get actual air and sunshine. We can take him to the park or somewhere close, roll him around some trails, let him stare at his birds. The kits need to hang out with their Granpop."

Margaret looped her arms around Samantha's shoulders.

"That would be lovely. We both need... something."

Hugging back, Samantha said, "Thanks for taking the kids. Just a few hours break is a relief."

It really was time they got moving. She had just shooed them out the door when behind her came, "Memaw, you make the best cookies. You know that? The *best*."

"And you waited for your mother to leave before telling me that," she said with a smile. "Let's go see what we have."

Cookies made, the oldest was content to sit in the living room with some little electronic thing thankfully keeping him quiet, and the youngest bounced on her lap while Margaret skimmed an online clothing site.

She pulled a face at each of the terribly tawdry outfits flashing far too much fur for her comfort. Did they all need to show off the belly like that? There wasn't a need to show off the extra twenty pounds she'd gained. "I just hope this isn't warping you," she cooed to the infant, who yipped and swished her tail in oblivious delight.

No, no maid. She didn't like that connotation. Both of them would laugh if she tried being a cheerleader. Finally a uniform inspired her. This site's offering didn't suit her, but after a bit of searching she found satisfying pieces on other sites. When the deliveries arrived she tested for fit in secret. Sending the white mini-skirt back had been a chore, but the replacement finished the affair. All that work piecing it together made a uniform better than any one outfit she'd seen. "Good job," she told her pleased reflection, turning to admire the ensemble.

She waited for an evening when Henry seemed at his best. Once the special night arrived, Margaret dressed and fussed over herself in the mirror. If she ignored the nervousness and the warmth of her ears, she supposed it looked well enough. The initial plan had been to wait for him to call for some errant need, but she couldn't wait around with the twittering sensation in her belly.

Margaret slipped into his bedroom and distracted herself with random tasks, waiting for him to look up from reading the paper.

The startled "What …." didn't take long.

She turned to find his ears high and eyes wide, full of surprised amusement and lust, along with something less pleasant she couldn't put her finger on.

Trying on her most lascivious smile, Margaret settled a hand on her skirt. "I remembered you said something about how nurses just don't dress the part any longer." The white uniform top bared little aside from its plunging neckline, hugging her tightly in an attempt to disguise some of the weight accumulated over the last few years. The skirt, though, showed nearly all of her stocking-clad thighs. "Is this better?"

"Very." He took off his reading glasses, no doubt to get a better look.

A fear eased inside of her. Dressing like a nurse might have offended him, reminding him of his situation and her role. From his smile she had no worries now.

Margaret leaned towards him and the little white hat fell to rest at the toe of her matching heels. "Oops. It just won't stay put." Stepping forward and turning her back to Henry, she bent at the waist and took her time retrieving the hat. The motion lifted her tail, and since she'd slid it under her skirt rather than through the tail-catch in the back, the skirt slid higher.

"I honestly can't remember the last time you dressed up," Henry marveled.

A rush of excitement bubbled up through her, reminding her of the early days of their marriage, the eagerness and new naughtiness of it all. Margaret giggled, actually giggled, and put the cap back on, perched precariously on the scarlet-going-grey bun of her hair. Any wiggle of her ears would disturb it.

"Now, I think I need to…give you a, uh…checkup." The sultry tone faltered as she frowned. Innuendo was something she next to never attempted, and here she thought it would have come naturally with the situation.

The sight of Henry tenting the sheet reassured her. She took her time setting the papers on his lap aside, touching him through the sheets in the process. After unveiling his penis she took hold and began to stroke. "Now, just relax back while I…while…just relax."

Apprehension wiggled about between her ribs, but she took a deep breath and ignored it. This was for him, after all. Leaning over the bed, Margaret ran her tongue along his tip. Oral sex had been a source of some friction earlier in their marriage, but it was easier for Margret to swallow her discomfort and swallow him on special occasions. Her lips brushed over him, intent on taking him inside.

"You don't need to do that."

"Oh, this is only to warm you up." Henry had never been one for multiple times, and she didn't want to waste this opportunity. She eased him into her muzzle and closed her eyes, giving the daintiest of sucks. The taste wasn't unpleasant. With the evening being so important, she pushed herself to bob vigorously, her tongue stirring along his length.

The vixen tilted, glancing sidelong up his body, and saw his face.

His face, with folded ears and eyes not looking at her, muzzle pursed like he held back a complaint.

Something broke inside of her. This had not been easy, and she was trying hard at making a last special event, trying hard to be the sexpot she had never been. And here he was, not satisfied?

Margaret lifted her muzzle and glared at him, the sharpness of her tone slipping past her control. "Am I doing this wrong?"

"No, that's how you're suppo—"

"Not this," she snapped and shook his penis at him, and upon realizing how absurd that looked, let him go. "I mean all *this*." The vixen straightened and gestured to her outfit, the bed, the room. "Am I boring you? Is this not, not ... slutty enough for you? You act like I'm doing it wrong! What do I need to do?"

"You need—" he halted and pulled the sheet over his lap, likely because his penis just bobbing there wasn't helping anything. "You need to *want it*." The last came out in a warbly choke, a raw ache she could see in his eyes. The intensity seemed to surprise him as much as her.

Margaret's ears went up before folding back. "What?"

Henry paused and swallowed, regaining himself. "When you jerk me off, you act numb, you do it like my orgasm is some chore to mark off a list. Just like when you do anything else for me. I would understand if it was uncomfortable, but if you're going to do it you should at least like it a little."

"I'm sorry but it's not exactly exciting for me to ...to... masturbate you."

"And this?" He gesturing to it all in much the same way she had earlier. "Sex, Margaret. Does this excite you? Because...because I can't please you like this. I can't. I'm a fucking cripple."

Normally her ears would have lain back from the coarse language, but the hateful loathing in his voice set them back now. "Don't say that," she said, her scolding tone failing to cover the lurching in her chest.

"Don't say the truth?" Something caught in his voice, and he looked away. "You cater to me in every other way, and I'm sorry you have to, I hate it, but I can't stand you doing this when it's just for me, when you should want it but you don't."

She knelt on the bed and leaned to touch his forehead

with her muzzle, her breath brushing his fur, to let him hide the glisten of wet eyes from her, and so he didn't have to see the drip of hers. Focusing on just holding him let her put her thoughts in order.

Serving as his nurse had been hard on both of them—it made them uncomfortable, it wore on her, it shamed him—but they'd talked and fought and dealt with that. It had never occurred to her the ALS had robbed him of his pride in their lovemaking too, in the attentiveness to her needs he had always shown. He knew she preferred him on top of her, and seeing what that fact did to him twisted her heart.

She would need to lie, a little, because there was some truth in it. Even now he hugged her, and it felt weaker than it should've. But she would be damned before she let him down.

Nuzzling between his ears put her lips close enough to murmur into one, "It's difficult, but not because of that. You've always been so good at leading, and I've enjoyed letting you enough that I never really learned how to be in charge. It feels awkward."

"Awkward is the mildest way I'd describe our life now." His voice's pitiful depth tightened her throat.

Sitting back, she gripped his shoulders and nearly touched noses. "Look at me. This isn't easy, but that doesn't mean it's awful. I love you and anything I can do to make you happy, and comfortable, and relaxed is a good thing."

"But you do so—"

She clamped her hand over his muzzle. "For just a moment, listen and don't talk. So my wanting to please you isn't good enough for you, fine. But right now, I do want to make love, because I want you." Unable to say the next bit while looking at him, she stared at his chest and said, "When you get worse, I won't be …comfortable with it then. I don't know how I'll feel when you can't move, can't touch me. But right now I am fine and I need you before I lose that too."

Leaning back, she slid her hand down his chest to cradle his package through the sheets. Now she looked up. "Right now, what I want is exactly what you've been giving me. I want to feel your touch all over my body. To have you against me, and enjoy what I can while you're able. Often." With her ears hot and the nervousness of his answer tensing her stomach, she asked, "Is that good enough for you?"

Henry's eyes sang. "Yes."

After a brief kiss Margaret sat on the edge of the bed, sliding her skimpy underwear down until they dangled from one stocking-clad ankle, just the way he liked it. She drew the sheet off him once more, but didn't straddle him until after he'd flicked the button to better angle the head of the bed, giving them more room.

Spreading her legs raised her skirt, making it quite easy to nestle the heat of her against his erection. Rather than put him in, she pressed herself in lazy rocking motions while watching his eyes.

"Are you teasing me?" he asked in amusement, working the buttons of her top loose.

Planting both hands above his head, she leaned and bumped his nose with her breasts. "No. I'm teasing the both of us."

One little lift, nudge, and drop let her begin to sink over him. It was enough to make him pause and close his eyes, and she watched him savor it until she settled on his lap. Only then did he nip at a freed breast. The flutter of his tongue to the nipple tightened her around him, left her shivering down to her tail-tip.

They were in no hurry and neither had the endurance for wildness, which suited Margaret for now. Rocking and stirring her hips always reminded her of using a hoola-hoop when she was a girl. While she didn't have the rhythm to keep the hoop going, here her coordination was just enough to keep them rolling.

Henry's touch. Like her hips, he moved with care, sometimes with only his palms, others the fingertips alone caressing through her fur or tracing a curve. Or he clung to her and squeezed like he couldn't get enough. Decades taught him what touches where left her panting. When he handled her like this Margaret felt like a prize, some cherished antique musical instrument he poured his heart into when playing. It always made Margaret give him an ovation, at least inside.

She would miss it. But she could see the intent behind it in his eyes, like how the desire to take her was there even when he couldn't thrust up to meet her. She missed that too, but would cope as long as they had each other.

Not that they had an entirely long time for tha-

No, she would not think about that, not now.

Henry took the distraction away. For several moments she had felt the beginnings of his knot brushing against her but now, as she pushed down to his root, there was enough thickness to cause resistance. Reaching up, her husband gripped the bun of her hair with what strength he had left. Margaret gasped. The little nurse hat fell off, instantly forgotten.

Whenever he drew close to tying, Henry became far more aggressive, and she used to give herself to him fully; wrapping legs around him and holding tight or arching her back while pressing her face into the mattress. Here though he could only grab her, show his desire to ravish her and she pushed for that wildness for him, rising to drop and slap her rump against his thighs. The crash of bodies helped wedge his knot in and she wriggled her hips, struggling more each time to slip free.

Henry yanked her hair a second time, forcing her lower. Fingers pushed under her hair and he grabbed at her scruff. The grip was sadly weak, not firm enough to flip that hot switch inside her, but it still sent a thrill up her spine, wringing a moan out of her. His own groan was lost in her breasts. Unable to take the tug of war any more, she shoved down. When it slotted in again, Margaret let his knot fatten inside of her, pressing against her insides, before she squeezed him and tugged with her hips.

A shudder ran underneath her. Even if he was lodged and going nowhere, Henry fought to thrust deeper but his body wouldn't cooperate. Margaret squirmed for him, pulling and squeezing the bulge inside of her. The knot blossomed, stubbornly cemented, and he burst inside her. Henry shook and she held him.

"Did you?" he gasped when the pulse of him inside her eased.

"No," she panted.

He let go of her hair. "Lean back."

Margaret tilted back until she could prop her hands behind her. His agile fingers dipped to the spot where their bodies linked, strumming her. This close to the edge, he easily rolled her right over.

In the moment she came, Margaret moaned deep in her chest, bounced her hips against his knot's tether, and let it all go. Discomfort, embarrassment, a ball of stress – for that brief time she was raw and wanton and nothing else mattered.

When it faded, she more or less flopped on him, panting into his neck. He held her.

In the warm haze, she smiled at the rumble of his chest as he spoke. "Margaret. I've been thinking."

"Uh oh."

"I had an idea of something we could try—"

"Henry, if you are going to ask me to do *that* I swear—"

"No, not that." He snorted. "How would you feel about tying me up?"

The vixen straightened and regarded him curiously.

"That's a little redundant, don't you think? Where else are you going to go?"

"Er yes, that's sort of my point. Me being too weak to touch you would make you uncomfortable, right? But if we tie my wrists up now while they can function, then later when they can't, you'll be used to the idea of them being bound and not touching you."

Her eyes narrowed playfully. "Have you always wanted to do this? Are you trying to nudge me into more?"

"Well…" With lowered ears he said, "I've wanted to tie you up for some time, but thought it would be too much to ask."

"I had thoughts of cuffing you to the table anytime we eat with my family. You always want to show up, eat and leave." Margaret chuckled and licked his nose. "It's very smart, and I'll do it if it can help." Perhaps it was the lingering release and tingling contentment, but a little ball of hope bubbled in her chest.

Henry cupped her rear. "I'll have to sacrifice much, but somehow I'll manage." He winked and squeezed. "You know, even when I can't use my hands, my muzzle is still quite agile."

"How lewd," she said with mock scandal, but kissed him. He showed her he was right.

"Now, how about we try th—"

A nip on the nose stopped him. "If I weren't attached to you, I'd now be walking into the hall."

"Well, then I suppose I should be thankful you're knot." Henry hugged her waist.

Having long since become immune to her husband's puns, Margaret gave him a tired smile and rested her muzzle on his shoulder, content. Even if the coming months were far from perfect, tomorrow's view looked far better than yesterday's.

About the Author

In 1997 a young Rechan stumbled into an AOL chat room full of furries. He never looked back. He has yet to find a community more welcoming, kind, or creative. Around the same time he started writing and after a year or two, was published in Silverfox's *New Furrotica* fanzine. Then Rechan became so embarrassed by the poor quality of his writing, he stopped writing until 2007. Things really took off from there, and here we are.

While he may write many sensual stories, Rechan is equally enthusiastic about horror, fantasy, all things supernatural, and pulpy action. Many of his stories have been published by FurPlanet, Sofawolf, and Rabbit Valley, but his attention has lately turned towards mainstream markets. Beyond writing and reading, Rechan loves puns, standup comedy, and politics is his passion.

He also finds it odd to be writing about himself in the third person, but given that you're still reading this, it must be turning out okay.

You might find him at a furry con sitting in or on a panel. The best way to find him though is Twitter; @rechanmole is his primary account, and his writing account is @molewords. Many stories can also be found on SoFurry or FurAffinity under the account "Rechan". Stop by and leave a comment, drop an email, say hello.

And always keep reading.